Praise for the Lila Maclean Academic Mystery Series

"A pitch-perfect portray   ing cast of
anxious newbies, tweed;   's as sharp
as they're wise. Lila's '   d to have
found. Roll on book two

— Catriona McPherson,
Multi-Award-Winning Author of the Dandy Gilver Series

"Takes the reader into higher education's secrets and shadows, where the real lesson is for the new professor—how to stay alive. If you're smart, you'll read this book."

— Lori Rader-Day,
Anthony Award-Winning Author of *The Black Hour*

"Entertaining, intricate, and oh-so-smart! The talented Cynthia Kuhn treats mystery lovers to an insider's look at the treacherous world of academia—seething with manipulation, jealousy, and relentless ambition. A terrific plot."

— Hank Phillippi Ryan,
Mary Higgins Clark Award-Winning Author

"A very intricate, cool story featuring the depth of an institution where everyone is dying to climb the ladder of success."

— *Suspense Magazine*

"Tightly plotted with a deliciously memorable cast of characters, *The Art of Vanishing* kept me guessing from start to finish, and Kuhn's smart sense of humor made every page a pleasure."

— Marla Cooper,
Author of the Kelsey McKenna Destination Wedding Mysteries

"Absolutely addictive."

— Kathleen Valenti,
Agatha-Nominated Author of the Maggie O'Malley Mysteries

"Whether Stonedale University English professor Lila is confronting a backstabbing colleague or investigating a murder attempt on a cantankerous bestselling author, readers will root for this enormously likeable heroine."

— Ellen Byron,
USA Today Bestselling Author of *Plantation Shudders*

"Smart, action-packed, and immensely satisfying, *The Subject of Malice* had me from page one. I love this series, and it just keeps getting better."

— Wendy Tyson,
Author of *Ripe for Vengeance*

"A pure delight from page one. Cynthia Kuhn's Lila Maclean mysteries will cure what ails you. Funny and fantastic."

— Becky Clark,
Author of the Mystery Writer's Mysteries

"A twisty mystery with a gentle, gracious humor and a touch of whimsy. Reading it is like spending the afternoon with a best friend. You laugh. You smile. And you want to see her again very soon. I can't wait for the next Lila Maclean mystery."

— Keenan Powell,
Agatha-Nominated Author of the Maeve Malloy Mystery Series

"Papers, and panels, and murder, oh my! Everyone's favorite professor, Lila Maclean (secret powers include reading and finding bodies), is back and she's on the case (officially)! Lila's latest adventure is full of high drama and high crimes. Such FUN!"

— Julie Mulhern,
USA Today Bestselling Author of the Country Club Murders

"An intelligent, witty mystery that will keep you guessing to the very end."

— Libby Klein,
Author of the Poppy McAllister Mysteries

**The Lila Maclean Academic Mystery Series
by Cynthia Kuhn**

THE SEMESTER OF OUR DISCONTENT (#1)
THE ART OF VANISHING (#2)
THE SPIRIT IN QUESTION (#3)
THE SUBJECT OF MALICE (#4)

THE SUBJECT OF
MALICE

THE SUBJECT OF
MALICE

A Lila Maclean Academic Mystery

Cynthia Kuhn

HENERY PRESS

Copyright

THE SUBJECT OF MALICE
A Lila Maclean Academic Mystery
Part of the Henery Press Mystery Collection

First Edition | July 2019

Henery Press, LLC
www.henerypress.com

Trade Paperback ISBN-13: 978-1-63511-511-6
Digital epub ISBN-13: 978-1-63511-512-3
Kindle ISBN-13: 978-1-63511-513-0
Hardcover ISBN-13: 978-1-63511-514-7

Printed in the United States of America

For my family (near and far)

ACKNOWLEDGMENTS

Heartfelt thanks to...

Henery Press, whose fabulous work has made this book possible.

The Hen House, House of Clues, Sisters in Crime, Malice Domestic, Left Coast Crime, International Thriller Writers, and Mystery Writers of America—for the community and inspiration.

Gretchen Archer, Jim Aubrey, Margarita Barceló, Mary Birk, Cindy Brown, Wendy Crichton, Annette Dashofy, Sandra Doe, Dorothy and William Guerrera, Elsie Haley, Sybil Johnson, Jennifer Kincheloe, Libby Klein, Dennis and Ursula Kuhn, Margaret Mizushima, Julie Mulhern, Barbara Nickless, Nora Page, Vincent Piturro, Keenan Powell, Renée Ruderman, Angela M. Sanders, Meredith Schorr, Craig Svonkin, Wendy Tyson, and Wendolyn Weber—for manuscript readings, generous words, and/or pep talks.

Chicks on the Case—Ellen Byron, Becky Clark, Marla Cooper, Vickie Fee, Kellye Garrett, Leslie Karst, Lisa Q. Mathews, and Kathleen Valenti—for all things blog-sister and way beyond.

Wonderful family, friends, and readers who have supported this series.

Ken, Griffin, and Sawyer—for your kindness, sunshine, and everything else.

Endless gratitude all around. xo

Chapter 1

At the door, I narrowly avoided a gray creature with tentacles waving every which way. In the lobby, I passed two formidable vampires arguing about coffins. Near the fountain, I glimpsed a trio of witches chanting over the water as if it were a cauldron.

Monster Night was upon us.

The gold banner behind the hotel registration desk welcomed guests to *Malice in the Mountains*, sponsored by the Horror and Gothic Society. The organization's first-ever conference was taking place near Stonedale, Colorado, where I was assistant professor of English at the university. Attendees had been invited to dress according to a daily theme and, as a result, the ensembles ranged from mild-mannered professor to full-on cosplayer. I had aimed for the former rather than the latter, choosing simple attire for a meeting with the editor of my first book.

Finding a vacant bench, I settled in to wait. Instrumental fiddle music played overhead, competing with the voices of enthusiastic scholars. It was an odd juxtaposition, but this was clearly no ordinary academic gathering, and the venue was part of the reason. The Tattered Star Ranch drew visitors from around the world to the foothills of the Rocky Mountains. Originally a working ranch, it had been used as a shooting location for many western films, but after it had begun to fall into disrepair in more recent decades, its ghost-town vibe had made it a popular location for horror movies.

When that era ended, new owners completed a costly expansion to transform the site into a full-service resort. The hotel proper was now U-shaped, with ten floors instead of the original three. Meeting rooms were situated in both wings with guest housing in the center. Along the back, a main street set left behind by one of the westerns had been converted into retail space. The middle of the square had been filled with gardens, benches, and statues. Wisely, the owners had played up the movie aspects—the entire place was dotted with leftover props and sets—and the hotel offered tours that sold out daily. Acres of forest surrounded the site, and a short walk over the wooden bridge spanning a babbling creek led to numerous hiking and horseback riding trails for those seeking additional adventure.

The renovation had yielded a lovely product. From where I sat, deep green pine trees were visible swaying in the wind through the glass walls. The seating was saddle brown and purposefully weathered, as if it had been plucked directly from the range. Rusted iron art pieces and mirrors with whitewashed frames were punctuated with yellow sunflowers. The stream of otherworldly characters passing by, however, would have looked more at home in an abandoned castle. I counted three werewolves, several wraiths, and a zombie.

I wondered if my editor would be in costume. I also wondered what we'd be talking about. Over a year ago, I had signed the contract with the university press and thrown myself into the work of getting the manuscript in order. Even though it was a revision of my doctoral dissertation on mystery writer Isabella Dare, much effort was required to reshape the material and perform additional research. The book was to be published in October, six months from now. The entire process—we had just completed final proofreading—had taken place over email. The only reason I was meeting Meredith Estevan in person was that we happened to be attending the same conference.

Her email invitation had been vaguely worded—she "wanted to go over some things." The materials I'd received so far had informed me that the press would sell primarily to libraries and academic audiences but would make the book available for general purchase as well. There was no mention of marketing strategies or any kind of events. I typed a reminder into my cell phone to ask her about my responsibilities as an author.

Author.

Still gave me a thrill, that word.

The late afternoon sunshine through the glass warmed my back, and I lost myself in a delightful daydream about launch parties and sold-out readings, even though I knew neither of those was going to happen for a book like mine. Scholarly studies didn't typically burst onto the scene in the same way as fiction. Unless you were a superstar. Which I was most definitely not.

"Lila Maclean." It was a statement, not a question. I recognized the voice immediately as that of my colleague and, though I wished things were different, archenemy.

Simone Raleigh stood before me.

Make that *two* Raleighs. Two sets of pearls, two tailored sapphire suits, two perfect blonde chignons—both exuding cool elegance and a sense of entitlement.

I snapped out of my daydream fast.

"This is my sister, Selene," Simone said, gesturing. "Remember I told you about her?"

Of course. Selene had applied for the job that I'd landed, setting up the foundation for my ongoing nemesis situation with Simone, who sought out ways to undermine me whenever possible, as retaliation.

"Nice to meet you, Selene." I extended my hand, which she

shook limply with her fingertips, seeming to want to avoid making contact with my skin. The gold bracelets on her slim wrist barely even moved.

"A pleasure. I hoped we'd run into you," she said in a clear voice, though her smirk conveyed amusement. "Simone's told me *so* much about you."

I had the distinct feeling that I'd just met Nemesis 2.0.

"Are you waiting for Merrie?" Selene smoothed her glistening locks. My own dark wavy hair was probably springing extra frizz just to rebel against being in proximity to such perfection.

"Merrie?"

Simone elbowed her sister, then sighed. "Meredith. The editor. She told us she'd be meeting you."

I looked back and forth between them. "You know her too?"

In response to my question, I was accosted by tinkling laughs from both sides.

"Of course. We went to school together—" Selene said in a reproachful tone that implied I should have known that.

"Yes, all in the same class, even." Simone addressed me. "Are you in your thirties too, Lila? Or perhaps a little older?" She pointed to the space next to her eye, suggesting that some hideous wrinkle had given away my secret.

Except that I didn't have any wrinkles there yet and she knew we had graduated from school the same year, which we discussed almost immediately when we were hired together. So I just nodded and put all my effort into not rolling my eyes, which would only hasten further development of my life markings.

"Merrie's the *dearest* friend—" Simone mused, sweetly. She said most things sweetly, which was a misdirection of epic proportions.

"Yes." Selene concurred in an equally syrupy tone. "And we haven't seen her in ages—"

"Simply *ages*. Far too long."

Selene turned to her sister. "When was it?"

"At the ski weekend—"

"No, it was the cruise—"

"Wait," Simone said, holding up one finger in victory, "it was the safari."

"Right! The safari."

They flashed beautiful white teeth at each other in celebration of having reached that agreement and faced me again.

"Anyway," Selene said, "I'm here to talk with her about my book. I've signed a contract with them, you know."

"How wonderful! Congratulations." I smiled at her. "What's your book about?"

"It's on an American writer that no one knows, and she's absolutely fabulous."

Very intriguing—I taught American literature as well. "What's her name?"

"Isabella Dare."

My body responded before my brain did, spiraling a stabbing pain through my midsection and spiking my heart rate. I stared at her stupidly, willing concepts to string themselves together into a response, but nothing happened. I looked down at my palms, which were damp from the adrenaline her words had sent shooting through my body, and concentrated on breathing.

Selene continued cheerily, "Have you ever heard of Isabella?"

Dragging my eyes up to her face was as difficult as if I'd been Sisyphus rolling a boulder uphill, but I counted it a small victory that I met her gaze steadily. I didn't say anything for a beat, and her face reddened. In that moment, I knew she was aware of what she'd done.

I nodded, then somehow managed to ask Selene—calmly—to tell me more about the book. She chattered on about her take, which was to compare Isabella's work to that of Charlotte Brontë.

"Isn't that your area?" I inquired of Simone, though I already knew it was. She'd made it very clear, from the day she arrived on campus, that Charlotte Belonged To Her.

"Yes. It is. How kind of you to remember." She dipped her head in a show of false humility. "I suppose you might say that my sister and I are writing this book together."

I couldn't speak for a moment. Simone, along with everyone in our department, knew that I was working on Isabella Dare. I'd not only talked about my work with colleagues, but also I'd presented on her writing several times at conferences—and all of our presentations were announced on the department website as well as compiled and circulated monthly in an email from our chair, Spencer Bartholomew, who was a kindly sort, prone to acknowledging faculty achievements.

The sisters watched me closely, waiting for a reaction. My shock had already transitioned into ice-cold rage, which, thankfully, kept me from shrieking like a gothic heroine who had just come face to face with a monster. Yet just when I thought I'd managed to regain my composure, a wave of dizziness swept over me at the realization that perhaps having coffee, for Meredith, meant telling me that they'd decided not to publish my book on Isabella Dare after all, since they had the one with the Raleighs. Which would translate into the fact that I either had to find another publisher, stat, or forget about keeping my job.

I reached down for my satchel in order to have something to do that didn't involve looking at the twins. While I was groping below the bench, I heard one of them exclaim, "Merrie!"

A petite woman strode over to us on the highest heels I'd

ever seen. She could have been a model, with shining black hair down to her waist and piercing blue eyes. Even through the lenses of her chic dark glasses, the power of her gaze made itself clear.

Simone and Selene wrapped her in hugs and expressions of affection while I stood there awkwardly, tapping my satchel. Eventually, Meredith tugged her fitted charcoal gray jacket back into place and looked over her frames at me.

"And who is this, please?"

The Raleighs gestured toward me in graceful slow motion, as though I was the prize revealed behind the curtain in a game show.

"Lila Maclean." I stepped forward and offered my hand.

"Oh! Just the woman I was looking for. I'm Meredith Estevan," she said, shaking my hand firmly. "I know we are scheduled for coffee in"—she consulted her oversized watch—"now, actually—"

"Couldn't we steal you away for a catch up?" Selene interjected, a wistful look on her face. "I'm sure Lila wouldn't mind talking business another time."

Adding insult to injury, as the saying goes. First, they steal my topic; now, they're going to steal my editor too? I raised my hand to object.

"We'll catch up later," Meredith assured Selene, then tilted her head. "How do you all know each other?"

"We're colleagues," I said. "Well, Simone and I are."

Simone threw her arm over my shoulder and smiled broadly. "Oh, we're more than that, Lila, aren't we?" She directed the next part to Meredith. "We started on the same day at Stonedale University—four years ago—and we've become very good friends."

We had?

Only if by "very good friends" she meant that I do the work

and she takes all the credit. Or that I dive into a project and she sabotages me. Like now, though it was sad to admit that it wasn't the first time she'd stolen an idea from me.

Meredith nodded thoughtfully. "And now you know Selene."

"We've just met," I said. Selene curved her lips up.

Simone put a hand on Meredith's arm. "We have *our* business meeting too, remember, Merrie." Then she shot a triumphant glance my way.

Message received. I knew she was completely aware of what she'd done. I also knew without a doubt that this was payback for Selene not having the job I currently occupied at Stonedale. But regardless of their motive, was there anything I could do about it? That was the question.

After they made arrangements, Meredith fixed her eyes on mine. "My boss has just arrived and he needs my assistance. I hate to ask, but could we speak before the panel tomorrow instead?"

We agreed to meet for breakfast on Friday morning, and I typed the time and place into my phone.

The three of them walked off together and I sank back down onto the bench.

I was in trouble. The kind of trouble that races toward you in the dark with unmistakable power.

Like a monster intent on your destruction.

Or a colleague with an agenda.

Chapter 2

At least I had somewhere to pace. I'd been gifted a bright, spacious hotel room for serving as a member of the conference site committee. All the hours of scouting locations and negotiating rates had been worth it. The cost of a single night at the Tattered Star Ranch would have cleaned out my bank account otherwise. I brought my suitcase up from the car and unpacked quickly. It was your typical bland hotel palette—taupe as far as the eye could see—though the wallpaper with a pattern of almost imperceptible stars added a touch of whimsy.

As I walked back and forth, carving tracks into the plush carpet, I went over the encounter with Simone and Selene in my head. There may have been some muttering involved. While I didn't reach any conclusions, the movement helped me burn off enough adrenaline to return my focus to the conference itself.

Hoping to chart a course through the weekend's activities, I settled down with the thick program and a yellow highlighter. My own paper was scheduled for tomorrow morning, so I marked that first. The sheer number of other options was overwhelming, and choosing panels wisely was key. Usually I felt obligated to go to anything that was even tangentially related to my areas of specialization—gothic and mystery—and ended up exhausted by the end of the weekend. And this time, given the conference focus, it seemed like everything was relevant.

Plus, in addition to panels, there were many other temptations. Did I want to go to The History of Literary Monstrosity Lecture? The Everything You Ever Wanted to Know About Sirens and Harpies Roundtable? The Obscure Weaponry Master Class? The Voices From The Grave Trivia Challenge? The Uncanny Costume Contest? The Build A Snare Workshop? The Final Girl Open Mic? The Make Your Own Cthulhu Mask Craft Bar?

Giving up for now, I dropped the highlighter, leaned back against the stack of pillows, and glanced at the clock. There was an hour until the welcome banquet started—plenty of time to make a call—and I needed to sort through what had just happened.

My cousin Calista, who was already a tenured member of my own department, answered breathlessly on the first ring. "I've been thinking about you! How is the conference going? Can't wait to get out there. Just need to finish up this work first. Writer on a deadline—well, you know how it is. How's the hotel?"

"The hotel is lovely, and the conference is only getting started, but you're not going to believe—"

"Hold on." I heard the sounds of paper rustling and a soft meow. "Just had to move Cady." Calista was putting together a new book of poems, and her beloved cat companion had a habit of settling down on the manuscript pages, which Calista tended to spread out on her dining room table. "Okay, I'm back, and I'm intrigued. What's going on?"

I filled her in on the conversation with the Raleighs.

She gasped. "You're kidding. That's...that's shocking."

The knot in my chest seemed to ease a little at her reaction.

"I mean, I knew she was working on a book on Brontë, but she never mentioned that Isabella Dare was part of it. That takes some nerve!" She launched into a tirade.

Her vehemence made me feel even more justified in my own response. I picked up the complimentary—they're complimentary, right?—pen on the nightstand and began to doodle on a blank page in the program.

Eventually, Calista coasted to a stop. "What happens next?"

"I don't know. I mean, the publisher didn't say outright that it was an issue, both of us having written on the same author, but I just have a bad feeling about it. I'm also wondering if I should even mention it? I mean, surely they already know. Maybe it's not a big deal."

"It's a big deal given that Simone absolutely, without question, is one hundred percent aware that Isabella Dare is your author."

"Isabella doesn't belong to—"

"You know what I mean, Lila. Simone *knows* that you have been working on this topic for years. And in that way, she is not showing you any professional courtesy at all by sneaking off to write on it too. It's shady."

"It definitely feels shady."

"That's because everyone in the department knows what everyone else is working on. Spencer has been terrific about circulating kudos in public."

"He really has—I thought about that too."

"My point is that what she's doing is outrageous. And I'm so sorry."

I let out a slow breath. "Can't even tell you how much I appreciate that. Thank you."

Over the line, I could practically hear Calista gathering steam. My cousin was fierce when she set her sights on a target. "Let's make a plan. We have to do something about this."

"What can we do? Simone and Selene have a contract with the publisher."

"Well, that may be the case, but I think that you should tell

Spencer immediately. Send him an email."

"I don't know. Isn't it going to sound awful, me complaining that a colleague has a book coming out? I mean, in all honesty, I'm happy for them in general—it's just the subject of their contribution that's got me riled up."

She was quiet for a moment. "I see what you mean. It might look like you're whining or something. Don't do it if you don't feel comfortable."

The doodle had taken on the shape of bookshelf with a pair of eyes peeking out from the shadows. Which might seem therapy-worthy on the surface, but I wasn't worried because pretty much the only things I'd learned to draw well in undergrad art class were eyes. We sketched them daily. My professor was obsessed with them. She always said that if we got the windows to the soul right, the rest would come eventually.

I was also good at drawing umbrellas for some reason. Not sure what that meant.

Calista said one more thing before disconnecting: "Rest assured, Lila, news about the Raleighs is going to get around, if you catch my drift."

After indulging in a bit more metaphorical gnashing of teeth, I went down to the Red Barn Event Hall—which had been relabeled "The Great Cavern" for the conference, according to my program—for the welcome dinner. Off to the left of the resort's town square, the newly constructed building was on the site of a barn that had burned down during one unlucky movie shoot at the ranch. It was twice the size of its predecessor and had the flexibility to be both banquet room and ballroom; the hotel manager had told me during our negotiations that it was already booked up for weddings three years out. We'd been able to snag it only because someone had just cancelled their nuptials ten minutes before I called about reservations.

A brief walk on a winding stone path led to the hall, which was set up with circular tables covered in white cloths for the hundreds of attendees. Mason jars with twinkling lights stretched across the room, hung in swaying lines below the huge wrought-iron chandeliers. At the far end was a wooden stage with hay bales stacked neatly in front of curtained wings. Servers were depositing salads onto the table, attendees were selecting their places, and the low buzz of conversation filled the space.

I was scanning the tables, looking for an open chair, when someone touched my arm lightly. A wave of powdery perfume hit me simultaneously, and I turned to find Meredith smiling at me, her hair shining under the lights.

"I'm so sorry I had to reschedule our meeting. You'll see why in a bit. I'm wondering, would you like to sit at the press table? We've saved you a spot." She gestured front and center.

I thanked her for the invitation and allowed myself to be towed along.

The other members of the table included Simone and Selene, who offered matching Cheshire Cat grins; a thin young man with spiky black hair and a gold nose ring; and a gentleman who very much resembled Alfred Hitchcock.

Meredith pointed to some open chairs. "Take your pick."

I slid into the seat next to Alfred Hitchcock and said hello. He gave me a nod but seemed otherwise indifferent to my presence.

As soon as Meredith had settled herself, she leaned forward and addressed him. "Richie, this is Dr. Lila Maclean. She's doing the Isabella Dare book for us. Lila, this is our managing editor, Richmond Haskin."

I caught my breath. Richmond was beyond famous. I knew that he ran the university press, but I didn't think I'd ever have the chance to meet him in person.

He clapped me on the back. "Good to meet you, Professor."

His hearty welcome was such a surprise in contrast to his initial demeanor that it took me a moment to respond. By then, he'd already gone on. "Glad you're with us. Glad to have you in the family. Glad to have you aboard. Just, you know, glad, glad, glad."

"Thank you very much," I said, smiling. "It's a pleasure."

"Oh, the pleasure is mine. All mine, I can assure you."

He picked up his fork and began to eat his salad, motioning with his other hand that we should do the same.

After a bite, he put down his fork and patted the thin man next to him on the back. "This is Hanover Jones."

He gave a wave of greeting with his fork and I did the same.

"Hanover," Richmond boomed, "is a bona fide genius."

The younger man humbly shook his head.

"He has taken our dusty little office out into the world on social media. Into the big wide world. The Instagram account is a work of art, I tell you!"

Hanover murmured a thank you and regarded Richmond fondly.

"You're going to be doing some great things for Lila here, aren't you, Han? Great things."

The social media genius nodded emphatically. "I've got everything planned. I'd love to go over the strategy with you later, if you have time, Lila."

I nodded enthusiastically. It was a good sign that they were talking about promoting the book. Maybe it wasn't dead after all.

Or maybe they were just pretending that it was going to be published until Meredith had the chance to deliver the news, so that it wasn't uncomfortable.

I heard a cough from across the table, which, although it

was tiny, screamed Look At *Me* Now. "Your Twitter account is also beautiful," Selene declared loudly. "It's the first thing I check every day. All of those quotes and images are an inspiration to those of us out in the field writing our little books."

"Me too." Simone's volume matched that of her sister. "Every day."

"And we can't wait to hear about what you're doing for *our* book." Selene smiled brightly.

The Raleighs weren't used to being out of the limelight.

And almost impossible to tell apart. Even though I'd worked with Simone for years, I wouldn't have been able to identify her for certain without her conference badge.

"We're excited about both of your books, of course," Richmond said. "We are looking at a banner year. A banner year, I say."

The sisters settled back into their chairs smugly.

This was going to be a long night.

Chapter 3

Two other people joined us, and the table exploded with introductions. Both were professors presenting at the conference: Ellis Gardner, a round, white-bearded man air who sported a dark suit and tie with mustard stain, and Candace Slaten, a slender blonde woman in a teal suit, who had multiple strands of gemstones looped around her neck. She smiled at me warmly. He was more interested in the tablecloth.

"We were just celebrating the press team, all of whom you already know," Richmond said to the newcomers. They nodded as he continued. "And finally, there's our Meredith, who edits like a dream. We'd be lost without her."

"Thank you, Richie," she said quietly.

Richmond returned to his salad.

I took a sip of the white wine that had just been placed in front of me by the server. "So is it just the three of you in the office?"

Meredith shook her head. "We have additional staff in acquisitions and editing, production and design, marketing and distribution—"

"We may be small, but we cover the bases, I assure you," said Richmond. "All the necessary bases."

"—plus several student interns who help out tremendously." Meredith said. "Bless them."

"And there's Dan," Hanover reminded her.

"Of course! Our office manager slash finance director slash superhero," Meredith said. "We would be lost without him."

"Here's to Dan." Richmond raised his wine glass. "And to everyone else at this table."

We all toasted. I already felt much better about working with this group.

If my book was still happening, that is.

It's true what they say about academia—it's publish or perish—so a lot was riding on this. And while I didn't own the topic, of course, I had been the only one working on Isabella Dare's novels for *years*. I'd done the research, so I knew there was nothing out there. No books, no articles, and no conference papers other than mine. I'd long dreamed of introducing her around. Not to mention that if the world found Isabella as important as I did, that was the kind of thing that could make a scholar's career.

Plus, I knew darn well that Selene Raleigh had not been working on Dare until recently; I'd heard that when she'd interviewed at Stonedale, she had been all about John Donne, mostly, and Robert Frost, barely. A member of the hiring committee had confided privately that she thought Selene had merely shoved the latter writer into the mix in order to appear qualified to teach American literature even though she didn't seem fully committed to the subject.

And Simone had outright mocked my topic in front of our colleagues the first time she'd asked me about my dissertation.

Something didn't add up.

Unless you factored in the part about Selene wanting the job that I'd gotten.

Then it made perfect sense.

They were out for revenge, pure and simple.

I took another sip of wine while the servers removed our salads and replaced them with a plate of butternut squash ravioli and grilled vegetables.

My thoughts tumbled forward. Ultimately, there was plenty of room for everyone to write on Isabella Dare. The most important thing was that we put the spotlight on her so that *could* happen. In fact, it wasn't that I didn't want anyone else to write about her—quite the opposite. I hoped that someday there was a veritable industry of scholars churning out articles and books on her work. It was that Simone and Selene were pretending they didn't even *know* about the work I'd done.

After they'd mocked me for doing it.

I sighed. Even if I wasn't happy with the intentional dovetailing onto my topic that I was sure had taken place, or the shady reason for it, their book would help support Isabella's importance.

And my book was scheduled to come out first, so at least there was that.

Turning my attention back to the discussion, I heard Selene say, "...and that's why we think our book should come out as soon as possible—say, September—instead of next February."

The silverware cut into my skin, as my hands curled into fists. Richmond, to my horror, was nodding. "Would it be too late to revamp the media schedule, Hanover?"

I willed him to say yes. He looked up at the ceiling and squinted. "I could probably make it happen," he said.

"Of course you could," Richmond said. "You're a genius."

Hanover smiled.

"But that would be a *complete* rush. We haven't even seen the finished—" Meredith interjected.

"Then it's settled," Richmond crowed, beaming at the twins. "Great, great, great."

I found myself standing without any recollection of having pushed my chair back. Eyes around the table looked surprised— except Simone's and Selene's. They were amused.

"Excuse me," I managed. "Be right back."

I made my way through rows of tables, stopping near the side wall to catch my breath. A server making his way to the kitchen in back paused to inquire if I needed help. I shook my head and thanked him. After giving me a concerned look, he hoisted the tray back onto his shoulder and went through the double doors.

When my heart had slowed to its usual pace, I went outside and called Calista. I recounted the conversation and listened to her response, which began with a string of curses aimed at the Raleighs, then veered into possible ways to let other people know how horrible they were, then coasted into potential retribution scenarios. When she finally reached the what-are-you-going-to-do-now phase, I was feeling much better.

"I'm going to talk to Meredith tomorrow," I said, resolving to be direct and unemotional. "We have a meeting and maybe she will see the—"

"Injustice!" Calista said angrily. "It's completely unfair."

"I was going to say issue, but okay, injustice, and maybe she'll revert to the original schedule."

"Your book should come out first, as planned. Being the first to publish on an obscure author holds more weight.

"But does it *always*? Maybe—"

"Stop. You have put in the work. You deserve to go first. Accept nothing less."

"I'll try to convince Meredith. If not, there's nothing else I can do."

"I'll keep thinking about it. Francisco might have some ideas." He might indeed. Her boyfriend was brilliant and determined.

Having vented, I felt capable of finishing the dinner now. "Thanks so much, Cal. How are you doing, by the way? Sorry I keep calling and dumping this drama on you."

"I'm fine. Just writing. And I *want* you to keep me posted. This is unbelievable. I'll be at the conference soon, but hang in there until then."

We said our goodbyes, and I took a deep breath, then returned to the table, hoping that the night would progress smoothly from now on. I couldn't take much more this evening.

Everyone was digging into their dessert when I slipped back into my chair.

"Lila, you must try the cheesecake immediately." Richmond waved his fork around and popped a bite into his mouth, as if he were playing airplane. "It's delightful."

I complied with his request and smiled at him. "It's delicious."

Although I tried not to look at the Raleighs, my gaze slid toward them when Simone made an expression of surprise. She was mouthing something to an individual at the next table and grinning.

"It's Beckett," she informed her sister. "We should have saved him a seat."

Selene squealed and jumped up from the table.

Simone soon stopped mouth-chatting and caught my eye. She looked down quickly. I wasn't sure how to read that.

However, when Selene returned, she stared, with a slow smile blossoming across her face. It was intended to signal her sense of victory, and it worked.

My stomach rolled over.

I faced my cheesecake again, no longer able to enjoy it, and set my fork slowly down on the plate. It was a relief to direct my attention to the stage when a sophisticated African-American woman in a burgundy suit walked over to the podium.

"Good evening," she said into the microphone. "I'm Acadia Branson, Chair of the Horror and Gothic Society."

Acadia, an academic superstar from Princeton, waited

politely until the applause subsided, then thanked the conference committee and the volunteers. She gave us a run-through of the main events and complimented those who had taken the Monster Night costume opportunity to heart. In keeping with the unique history of the hotel, she explained, the theme for the keynote dinner on Friday was The Old West, and the theme for Saturday's Awards Gala would be Literary Figures, with both character and author costumes welcome. The keynote speaker had not yet been announced, and the conference program had warned us to "buckle our seatbelts," whatever that meant. It was unusual for a keynote not to be named and advertised far in advance, as that could be quite a draw for attendance, but it also lent an air of mystery, I had to admit.

Next, she introduced all of the nominees for awards that would be given out at the Gala—a long list of scholars paraded up the stairs, across the stage, and back again after receiving their certificates suitable for framing from a beaming Acadia. Following that came the winners of the graduate student scholarships. They bounded earnestly onstage, one by one, and stood there twinkling shyly at us while she finished handing out the attractive wooden plaques. It felt as though things were rolling to a close when Acadia said, "And now we have a surprise for you. May I please have Richmond Haskin and company join me?"

He pushed his chair back slowly and waited for Ellis and Candace to do the same. They proceeded to the stage.

I looked questioningly at Hanover, who winked at me before turning to watch his boss. It was a tribute to his reputation that Acadia didn't even have to name the press; everyone knew the name Richmond Haskin. He had been an extremely prolific scholar during his time at various Ivy schools—he'd been wooed from one to another regularly—and he was famous not only for his monographs but also his edited anthologies focusing on a specific topic and bringing together a variety of scholars. He had been lured to Fairlake University, a small private school on the east coast—very much like Stonedale—by the opportunity to launch his own press about a decade ago. From the beginning, he'd chosen cutting-edge topics and seemed to stay just ahead of the curve.

"Greetings, colleagues," Richmond said into the microphone. "Thank you for your attention. As you know, Fairlake is a small press, but we have painstakingly built a strong reputation. That's due to the incredible work of our authors."

He bowed his head as applause swept the room.

"We have two announcements for you, actually. As you know, the conference awards will recognize the best that has been published during this past year. We've just heard the names of the finalists in all the categories. Congratulations to you all!"

There was more polite applause.

"The Horror and Gothic Society has allowed us to add a new award to the mix: the Fairlake New Voices Prize. Every year, we will select the best proposals that have been submitted to our press. Those authors will be on a special panel at this conference, which we hope will continue for many years." He smiled broadly at Acadia. "The winner will be chosen by a board of judges who attend the special panel on Saturday. They'll base their decision on a review of the proposal along with their evaluation of the scholar's performance at the panel, which will include a brief reading from the manuscript as well as responses to selected questions. The winner will be announced at the Gala."

He pulled a sheet of paper out of his pocket. "Please join me onstage if you hear your name. And audience members, do hold your applause until I complete the list. This year's finalists are Beckett Standhouse for his project, *War Imagery in the Work of Flynn McMaster*; Simone and Selene Raleigh for *Brontë and Dare: Double Trouble*; and..." he paused dramatically as the twins squealed and hugged each other. "Lila Maclean, for *Beyond the Veil: Isabella Dare and the Gothic.*"

I froze and looked at Meredith.

She was smiling and nodding. "Yes, Lila. Go up there."

I made my way dizzily toward the stage, shaking my head slightly, trying to clear it. Nothing was making sense.

The audience continued to applaud until we were all in a line next to Richmond. He made his way down the row, handing each of us a certificate and shaking our hands, then returned to the microphone. Acadia shepherded us over to the side, where it took all my effort not to sink down on a hay bale. As if it weren't surreal enough to be onstage in the first place, the sight of the crowd turned it up a notch. From this vantage point, it was easier to see the wide range of costumes—from someone who had simply donned a t-shirt that read *Nevermore* and perched a stuffed raven on his shoulder to a larger-than-life Headless Horseman, complete with flowing cape and glowing pumpkin tucked beneath his arm.

Richmond rubbed his hands together. "And now for the second surprise. We are very excited—thrilled, frankly—to announce that our press will be publishing a new series of critical guides on contemporary gothic and horror writers. Intended for professors, researchers, students, and general readers alike, they are going to be very valuable to your work. Each book will focus on an author and include four types of materials: several essays, a detailed biography section, a collection of interviews, and relevant photographs of the author's life."

He waited until the round of applause died down, then

smiled. "Tonight, we kick things off with our first guide, on one of the best and brightest: Flynn McMaster."

The room went wild. An English professor-turned-bestselling-author, Flynn McMaster was extremely popular, both with mainstream readers and scholars in literary studies and popular culture. Each of the six books in his series featuring Dr. Powell Block, a scholar-warrior-detective doing epic battle with various paranormal creatures and monsters, had catapulted to the top of the bestseller lists since his debut. Several chartbusting feature films had already been made with all-star casts, and several more were in the making. His books crossed genres and appealed to fans of fantasy, horror, gothic, and mystery.

Eventually, Richmond was able to continue. "The materials have been carefully curated for your use and enjoyment. I can vouch for the quality, as I had the great honor of editing this collection, along with Ellis Gardner and Candace Slaten, both colleagues of mine at Fairlake University. Several talented scholars contributed essays, and I'd like to introduce them now. Please hold your applause until the end, shall we?" He looked sternly around the room, then reeled off several names: Sharita Dawes, Lawrence Ling, Topher Armitage, Nan Delancey, and Winston Hughley.

As the audience applauded, he handed the microphone to Acadia, who informed us that we could buy our own copy in the book room immediately following the event. In addition, she told us there would be a signing with the editors and essay contributors on Friday afternoon.

"And on that note," Richmond added gleefully, "it's time to meet your keynote speaker. Please welcome Flynn McMaster."

The applause was deafening. From a curtain behind the hay bales on the opposite side of the stage, a tall, handsome man emerged. His long brown hair was gathered into a messy knot at the back of his head, and he wore a white tunic over black leather pants, accessorized with multiple pendants and bracelets. It was all very rock and roll.

Flynn moved quickly across the stage and shook hands with everyone before stepping up to the microphone.

"Hello," he said with a little wave, setting off an avalanche of claps and whistles.

Once the commotion had died down, he grinned and gestured to the professors alongside him. "Many thanks to everyone here. It's quite an honor to have your work considered..." His hands flailed as he searched for the right word.

Richmond leaned into the microphone and said "important."

Flynn tipped his head down in acknowledgment. "Thank you, sir."

Richmond continued. "Yes, your work is *very* significant, Flynn. So say we all. And," he turned to the crowd, "we know you can't wait to get your hands on this gem. So we've prepared a little experience for you. Follow the signs out front. They will lead you to your opportunity to be among the first to purchase a copy of this groundbreaking guide."

Murmurs broke out around the room and continued as Arcadia wished everyone a good night. I thanked Meredith for the invitation to sit with the press and followed Hanover outside to where large signs were displayed along the path back to the main building. There were multiple pictures of Flynn McMaster on easels in various authorly poses, one with all three editors standing rather stiffly in a group and smiling at the camera, and one of the contributors crunched together in a circle and holding a book above their heads. Inside the hotel, we were ushered into a large rectangular room with a "Book Lair" sign. The horror theme of the conference was admittedly straining a bit against the cheery ranch-chic remodeling touches, but that just made it more interesting.

Tables were piled high with the guides, as well as Flynn's other books, all ready for purchase. I paused at the end of the line that already snaked around the outer perimeter; looked like the entire dinner population had come directly to the book room, as directed. After twenty minutes or so, during which I checked work emails on my phone and only progressed about three feet forward, Hanover appeared.

"Have you seen the guide yet, Lila?"

"No. I didn't want to hold it the whole time I was in line."

"They're selling so fast you might not get one otherwise." Hanover took a few steps away, to the nearest table, then returned with a hardcover book, which he handed to me. "You better hold on to this. Don't want you to miss out. Also, I'm dying to hear what you think. You know what they say...first impressions and all that. Could you please take a look and let me know your thoughts? Do you like the layout? Is it easy to navigate? And so on."

I thanked him and looked down. The cover was in a lurid crimson, with the title splashed across the front in an antique sort of script, *Go Ahead and Scream: A Critical Guide to the Work of Flynn McMaster*. I opened the cover to read the first page.

Just then, a high-pitched scream pierced the room.

Chapter 4

For a split second, I thought the book had a soundtrack, like one of those birthday cards that plays a song when you open it.

But when the room went silent, I knew it had come from somewhere else. Hanover and I stared uneasily at each other for a long moment. People were conferring behind us, trying to figure out what was going on.

Meredith burst through a side door, near where we were standing. She waved her hand frantically at us to come over. "Where's Richmond?"

"I don't know," Hanover replied.

She looked at me and I shook my head as well.

"Call him and tell him to come," Meredith said to Hanover. "Quickly."

We followed her into the next room, where CPR was being performed on someone. From my angle, all that was visible were two trousered legs, which were parallel and unmoving.

"It's Ellis," Meredith whispered loudly.

"Did you call 911?" Hanover asked.

"Yes. They're still on the line." Meredith pointed at Simone, who was standing off to the side, talking on her cell phone.

"What happened?" I asked Meredith softly.

"I don't know. After the announcement, Richmond wanted me to check on some details with the event manager, which I did, down in the barn. Ellis had already left. When I returned,

Simone and I headed to the book sale together. We were just using this room as a shortcut to avoid the line, and we found him like this. It was dark and I tripped over him. When Simone turned on the lights, and I saw the blood, I screamed before I could help myself."

"There's blood?"

"On his head and the carpet next to him."

I surveyed the room. Chairs were set up in rows for audience members facing two long tables at the front that would accommodate the speakers of a future panel. One of the chairs nearby was turned on its side, but nothing else looked out of place. "Was there anyone here?"

"No. Just him." Meredith shivered. "I have no idea how this could have happened—" She broke off at the sight of the paramedics racing through the doors.

We watched them take over.

"Can I get you anything? And we should have the paramedics check you out too."

She shook her head, rubbing her arms, eyes fixated on the revival attempts. "I just want to stand here."

The doors opened again and I sighed in relief.

"Who's that?" Meredith said, following my gaze toward the man with cheekbones so sharp they could leave a scratch, spiky dark hair, and a purposeful stride.

"Detective Archer from the Stonedale PD."

He had his notepad out by the time he reached us. He gave me a quick nod and started asking questions. Meredith didn't seem surprised to see a detective there, though some might have wondered why he'd been called.

Truth was, he was already at the hotel to see me.

We'd been a couple since the fall of my third year as an assistant professor. I was in the spring of my fourth year now, so we were at the year and a half mark. It was hard to believe that we'd met while he was investigating a crime and I was the one who was suspected of having committed it.

Or maybe it wasn't hard to believe.

People meet in all kinds of ways.

But one thing was for sure: Lex took life seriously. He had a light side too, but his job mired him in the kinds of horrific things that people could do to each other on a daily basis, so he had cause for a somber outlook.

I never tired of seeing him in action.

Or inaction.

Just seeing him, period.

Because it had happened in an otherwise-unoccupied room and because the hotel staff had been able to direct the paramedics and police into and out of the room using a back hallway, not many people knew exactly what was happening yet.

Meredith asked us to keep things as quiet as possible.

Meanwhile, the book sale proceeded as planned. There was no chance of that not going forward. I'd never seen more people intent on purchasing the same book in one room. And there was no chance of the conference being cancelled, either, I suspected. People had come from all over the country—in some cases, the world—to present at this event. Unless the police decreed that the conference be ended, it would soldier on.

But Meredith was a wreck. It had taken her a long time to stop shaking, and Simone and Selene eventually led her into the hotel bar, presumably in search of something to calm her nerves. I'd trailed behind, not knowing what else to do. Although my first choice would have been to stay as far away from the Raleighs as possible, I wanted to support Meredith.

I decided to grit my teeth, summon my most professional self, and pretend they weren't completely beastly. Some wine would help with that.

We had a round of drinks and speculated about what could have happened to Ellis. After an hour or so, Meredith received a text. I watched her face crumple and knew Ellis was gone even before she told us. Someone had hastened his demise, she said, judging from the bar of metal they'd found underneath his body and the bar-sized gash in his head.

Little by little, despite the efforts toward discretion on the hotel's part, word got around. The circle at our table in the bar grew, with the addition of more and more scholars who had questions. No one seemed to have any idea who could have done it.

Candace eventually joined us, setting her drink down too hard on the table. It sloshed over. I handed her the paper napkin from beneath my empty glass, which she acknowledged with a small smile. She dabbed at the spill with one hand while she wiped at the tears welling in her eyes with the other.

"Were you very close?" I asked.

She rummaged in her bag and retrieved a tissue, which she used to pat her nose delicately. "I've known him for years, ever since I was hired at Fairlake. And working on this book together—it strengthened our relationship, you know?"

"So you were close?"

"Do you mean..." she appeared vaguely shocked. "No. It wasn't romantic. I mean, first of all, he's almost seventy. I'm only forty-one."

"That's not what I meant—"

She tapped a long fingernail on the table. "Second, I've been married for ten years. Ellis was just a friend. But a dear man."

I nodded. "I'm very sorry for your loss."

"Thank you." She wiped at her eyes again and swore softly under her breath. "I just can't seem to stop crying."

"It's understandable, Candace." Wanting to give her some

privacy, I offered to buy her a refill of her vodka soda, which she accepted, and I went up to the counter. When I looked back, she was biting her expensive manicure to shreds.

Later, I read my paper aloud in my room. I was glad that it had been finalized before I came to Tattered Star Ranch; there was no way I could have written—or even edited—it, considering the state of mind I was in now. But I'd worked hard before I left home, carefully developing what I hoped was a thought-provoking argument about Isabella Dare's use of symbolism. Reading the familiar words aloud was steadying, even comforting, after the events of the evening.

When I reached the end, I checked the timer. Perfect. We were allotted fifteen minutes each, and I was just under. All four of us would give presentations, then there would be a question-and-answer period at the end. I hoped that our session would be animated. On previous panels I'd been on, most people read their papers aloud. A few had talked from notes or lists, but while some were a triumph, others were a total disaster. It depended on the skill of the speaker. The audience was a factor too—they may listen extremely closely or barely at all, depending upon their level of interest in the topic.

The nerves hadn't kicked in yet, but I was experiencing the sort of awkward hopefulness that typically appeared when I attended a gathering of scholars. You never know whom you might meet. Someone who could change your career trajectory. Or someone who might challenge your paper's thesis in front of a room full of professors. It could go either way.

A soft knock interrupted my musings.

When I pulled opened the heavy wooden door, Lex gave me a weary smile. His tie was loosened and his notepad was sticking out of his suit pocket at a crooked angle.

"Professor."

"Detective."

He gave me a quick kiss and went over to the bed, where he sat down.

"Are you okay?" I tried to measure his energy with a glance.

He shrugged. "Always a tough day when we lose someone."

I nodded and sat down next to him, rubbing his back.

Lex gave me a grateful look and pulled his tie the rest of the way off.

"Want to talk about it?"

"No, thanks." He fixed his blue eyes on mine. "We don't know much. Yet."

I didn't tell him that word on the street—a.k.a professors in the bar—had already delivered information about what had happened to Ellis. Lex obviously needed a break.

"Just want to sit here with you."

"We can do that." I handed him the tv remote.

He chose a sports channel and moved up so as to be able to lean against the headboard. I scooted up next to him and put my head on his shoulder.

I woke up in the same position, with both arms asleep and a giant crick in my neck. Grimacing, I eased myself away, then did some stretching in the hopes of getting my blood moving. A shower helped a little.

When I emerged, feeling halfway human again, Lex was gone and there was a note saying he'd call later and he hoped I'd have a great day. It also told me to be careful.

That was lovely but I didn't travel in the same circles as Ellis Gardner, so although I was sad about what had happened to him, I wasn't too worried about danger coming my way.

Then it struck me that perhaps I did travel in the same

circles as Ellis Gardner, sort of, given that we'd shared a table at dinner last night.

Now I was a bit more worried.

I pulled on a black jacket and long skirt, braided my dark hair, and added some dangly silver earrings. A quick swipe of lip gloss and I was ready to head downstairs for the breakfast meeting with my editor.

It would be tricky to speak to Meredith about my concerns, since she and the Raleighs were, according to the sisters, chums from school. I'd have to be my most democratic. In the elevator, I tried to think of ways to raise the issue and came up short. I'd have to wing it.

With a soft chime, the doors opened, and I headed around the corner toward the restaurant. The Path's End was popular with locals and guests alike for its delicious, ever-changing menu and for its terrace overlooking the Rocky Mountains. Meredith was at a table next to the window, studying papers stacked neatly in front of her. The jagged peaks in the background were bathed in sunlight but retained snow.

When I arrived, she gestured to a silver carafe resting on the white tablecloth. "Would you like some coffee?"

"More than anything in the world."

She smiled and poured me a cup while I stowed my bag on the seat next to me and unfolded the orange napkin on my plate, which had been fashioned into a swan.

Or a duck. Something birdlike, anyway.

I took a long drink of the coffee, feeling its rejuvenating effects immediately. A smiling blonde woman in a pinstriped vest took my order and melted away, as Meredith picked up the papers and tapped them a few times on the table to align them before sliding the stack into the briefcase next to her chair.

"How are you doing? Any word on what happened to Ellis?"

She shook her head and tightened her lips. Her suit was a

dull brick shade, which emphasized the redness of her eyes. I wondered if she'd slept.

"I'm so sorry again, Meredith."

She took a sip of orange juice. "I appreciate that, thank you. Sorry I was a bit of a mess last night."

"No apologies necessary. It must have been awful to find Ellis like that."

"It was. Hopefully we'll have some answers before too long."

"Did you know him well?"

"Just as an editor on this project. He and Candace did come to the office a few times for meetings with Richmond, but they did a lot of the work via email or elsewhere on campus. From what I could tell, he was a smart, hard-working man. Not the most friendly person I've ever met, but Richmond admired him. I think they grew up together or something."

"Any idea about who could have wanted to hurt him?"

Meredith stared past my shoulder, her gaze unfocused. "No idea at all, but I'm wracking my brain." Her eyes wandered back to meet mine and she straightened up. "Shall we get to the matter at hand? First of all, we're very excited about your book. Such a wonderful subject. Second, congratulations on being a finalist for the New Voices award."

"Thanks so much, Meredith." Every muscle relaxed just a little. Ever since hearing about the Raleighs' book, I'd slipped gradually into the worst-case scenario.

She bent back to her briefcase and withdrew a leather portfolio. Removing a single sheet, she handed it to me across the table. "Here's the marketing plan. Please take a look and let me know if you have any questions."

I studied the schedule as the server returned, moving sideways to allow her to set down a white plate holding a slice of quiche and fresh fruit in front of me and a grapefruit half with a cherry on top in front of Meredith.

That's why she was shaped like a model and I...wasn't.

"I'm excited about this project, Lila. The way you described Isabelle Dare as a cross between Shirley Jackson and Agatha Christie—with a twist—caught my attention right away," Meredith said, loading her spoon with the cherry. "How did you become interested in her writing?"

I told her the story of finding Isabella's books in a dusty box at a New York City bookstore during grad school, reading and falling in love with them, then fighting to persuade my professors to allow me to write a dissertation on an author they'd never heard of. That had taken months of convincing, but eventually, they'd given me permission and I'd spent the next few years writing the dissertation that would become the foundation for the current book.

She nodded approvingly. "I knew you'd have an interesting discovery story."

"Oh, I like that phrase, 'discovery story.'" I rested the page on the corner of the table and picked up my fork to sample the quiche, which was delicious. "Did you ask Selene the same thing?"

I was, needless to say, eager to hear the answer.

"Yes. Her story was not as remotely interesting as yours. She said she heard someone give a paper at the Modern Language Association conference two years ago and was inspired to research further."

That was a lie. No one had presented on Dare at the MLA conference. I'd spent hours combing the session lists each year to see if anyone had done that very thing. I debated telling Meredith but decided not to say anything.

She dug into her grapefruit and expertly extracted a section. After she swallowed the triangle of fruit, I leaned forward.

"I do have one question..." Might as well get it over with.

"Yes?" She set the spoon down and looked up at me, a pleasant expression on her face.

"Would it be possible to..." I trailed off. This was harder than I thought. I didn't want to sound as though I were complaining about her friends. Even though that was the gist of it.

I had to try another tack.

One that didn't name the Raleighs outright.

I shifted in my chair. "Remember last night, when the schedule was changed?"

"Yes..." She went for another grapefruit section.

"Well, does it need to be changed?"

She paused. "Do you have a problem with it?"

"Well..." I couldn't think of a way to finish the sentence that conveyed *Yes! I've worked toward this for years and they just showed up and cut in line! Who does that? It's completely unfair!* without using any of those words, and I ended up shrugging.

So far, this was going *super* well.

Meredith regarded me thoughtfully.

I stabbed at a strawberry, my face aflame.

She slid her grapefruit to the side of the table and laced her fingers together in front of her. "Lila, I'm your editor. We need to be able to trust each other, so please speak freely."

I hesitated. "It's a bit delicate."

"Is it about Simone and Selene?"

I stared at her.

She laughed. "When you've been around them for decades, as I have, you know that it's *usually* about Simone and Selene. They have a way of steamrolling over everyone else once they get their minds on something. And between you and me, what they want often involves what someone else has already achieved. Are you aware of that dynamic?"

"I am aware."

She continued briskly. "Believe me, I've been in their crosshairs before too. I recognized the signs. They're relentless."

I wanted to hug her but refrained.

"Now. Straight talk. I know you are an expert on Isabella Dare. The depth of your knowledge is clear in the book, especially when you put it next to theirs." She frowned. "Maybe that's not fair. I haven't actually seen the second half of their book, which Selene is writing. I've only seen Simone's half, which discusses Brontë as a gothic writer and sets up the context for the comparison to Dare, with only very fleeting mention of Isabella. Their proposal indicates that Selene will be developing connections in the second half. She's supposed to deliver it to us this weekend. So I haven't seen much specificity. Yet, anyway. I remain hopeful."

I nodded.

"But I know that it matters in terms of scholarship which book comes out first. I'm sorry that we didn't discuss this more last night, but they—not to put too fine a point on it—basically blindsided us at dinner. I was more focused on the logistics of changing the schedule initially than on the implications of the request. Plus I was nervous about not saying anything to ruin the news about the McMaster book launch and the award. So I was distracted. Please forgive me."

"There's nothing to forgive," I hastened to reassure her. "And thank you for the nomination—I'm still stunned."

She smiled. "I'm happy for you. Anyway, it struck me after dinner what seemed to be going on, and how this would affect you, so I mentioned it to Richmond. We were going to talk with you after the book sale, but then when we went to the book room..." she shook her head.

"Ellis."

"Yes."

Meredith looked down at the table for a long moment, then raised her head. "In any case, rest assured that if you're interested, we are more than ready to publish yours in August. The month before theirs. We are way ahead on your project, anyway. I mean, we've already done the proofs. The least we could do is shift the print date."

My heart leapt. I pointed to the sheet she'd given me.

"We'll adjust that schedule too. Hanover won't mind."

"Thank you, Meredith. I...I don't know how to express how grateful I am."

"No need."

"I was so afraid—"

"That I was in cahoots with Simone and Selene?" She grinned.

"Exactly."

Meredith lowered her voice. "No way. Has Simone made your life miserable at Stonedale?"

"In a thousand ways."

She nodded at my plate. "Let's enjoy our breakfasts and exchange horror stories about the Raleighs."

So we did.

Chapter 5

I gave my paper on Isabella Dare shortly after breakfast. The three other professors who gave papers were fascinating—well, two of them were. The last professor, on the other hand, read so softly that none of us could hear what he was saying. From the first wave of This Is Excruciatingly Awkward that swept the room, through the Seriously What Is He Doing Up There stage, into the final We Have All Given Up Hope Of Understanding phase, we rode it out valiantly together and clapped in relief when it was over.

Our question-and-answer period was lively, and no one hurled any questions at me that I couldn't answer. That's always a possibility, given that conference panel questions can range from a genuine inquiry presented by an interested listener, to a rambling monologue designed to highlight the expertise of the asker that in no way requires your participation, to an outright challenge from someone who feels territorial or just enjoys skewering other scholars.

As the audience moved toward the exit, several people came up and told me that they'd enjoyed my paper. Couldn't ask for anything more than that.

Selene and Simone had attended but hadn't made eye contact; they'd been scribbling notes the whole time. I wasn't sure what to think about that, but I knew it probably wasn't something beneficial.

At least to me.

But my paper was done. Now I only had to worry about the surprise-you're-on-another-panel event that had been scheduled for Saturday. I hoped they'd give us more details before we walked into the room, but who knew what the plan was. I should have asked Meredith, but I'd been so focused on delicately presenting my argument for changing the schedule that I didn't have any remaining bandwidth to accommodate anything else.

After packing up my bag, I walked across the crowded hallway and into the lobby, with the goal of buying a latte to fortify me for the next session. I had almost reached the conference attendees waiting for their coffee fix when I saw Simone and Selene speed up in order to get in line ahead of a white-haired woman who was moving slowly and determinedly in that direction. They raced past her so quickly that she was knocked off balance, and I rushed forward to grab her arm and help her right herself. Then I invited her to go ahead of me.

"Thank you, dear." Her green eyes were similar in shade to my own and she seemed oddly familiar. "Thought I was going down for a moment there."

"Are you okay?" Despite her cheery tone, I was concerned.

"I'm fine," she said, chuckling. She tugged her yellow cardigan down over a long, flowered skirt that almost reached her blue sneakers and smoothed her white hair back into a neat bun. "It just gets a little harder to stay upright when you get on in years, you know. I'm not usually this slow, but the polish on this floor is a fall waiting to happen, so I'm just being careful."

"You're right—it's very slippery."

"And of course it doesn't help when people like *that* cut in line." She jabbed a thumb at the Raleighs.

Truer words were never spoken.

"Enjoying the conference? I am. It's been ages since I attended any professional gathering. But I was poking around the web and discovered this event. I was very intrigued by some of the topics here. I enjoyed your paper, by the way."

The sense of familiarity clicked into place—she'd been in the back of the room, nodding along with my presentation, even smiling at some points. In other words, she was the sort of audience member one dreams of.

"That's so kind of you. Thanks for attending the panel."

We exchanged credentials—she was Bibi Callahan, retired professor of literature—and fell into a conversation during which I went on a bit about Isabella, as I am inclined to do, and she held forth on Agatha Christie. The chit chat was enough to keep us entertained until we had our drinks in hand. Then we wished each other a good day and went our separate ways.

I was convinced of one thing: if the Raleighs were willing to knock someone down to get to their cappuccino faster, I needed to be careful. Especially once they found out that their little rescheduling plot had failed.

I attended two other panels—"Twenty-First Century Urban Gothic Themes" and "Ghost Sightings in Recent Film and Media Studies"—and enjoyed them immensely. My body was tired from sitting, but my brain was sparking; listening to others talk about their topics proved rich in catalysts.

Wandering into the lobby, I found an open spot next to the fountain and sat down to wait for Lex. We had planned to go into Stonedale to grab a bite and take a little break from the wall-to-wall scholars. Also, and he didn't know this yet—or maybe he did, as he knew me pretty well—I fully intended to find out what he knew about Ellis.

Richmond slid onto the bench next to me, breathing heavily.

"Are you all right?" He was pale and his forehead glistened.

"I am indeed," he said absently, as he looked over his shoulder at the crowd. "Just taking a moment out. You know how dreadful these things can be. Everyone wants something, every minute. One gets tired of smiling. It's exhausting."

He removed a monogrammed white kerchief from the pocket of his brown suit and patted his face. "There. All better." Then he tilted his head. "Who are you meeting? Your perfume is lovely."

I blushed. "It's tea rose essential oil. I'm surprised you can smell it—I applied it hours ago."

"I have a very keen sense of smell," he said. "Very keen indeed. Which is both a blessing and a curse as I'm constantly assailed by anyone walking by. And taking the bus is misery, quite frankly."

"I can imagine. By the way, I'm so sorry about Ellis."

He nodded gravely, staring at the ground. "It is a great loss to us all."

"How long have you known him?"

"Forever and a day. That's the long and short of it. We grew up in the same town. Became friends when we were just knee high to a cricket. Eventually went off to different schools but we remained close." He blinked rapidly—I could see that his eyes were full of tears. "Very close."

Time to change the subject—slightly, anyway.

"How are the book sales?"

He brightened and put both of his hands on his knees, squinting up at the ceiling as if he were calculating his gains. "Splendid. We sold out last night and had another shipment overnighted for the book signing later today. You'll be attending, I presume?"

"Looking forward to it."

"Good. I'd like to introduce you to Flynn. You're both our authors now. I suppose precision demands that I call Flynn a *subject* of our books, but in any case, we're all associated, and Fairlake is glad to claim you both as our people in whatever manner we can."

A thrill shot through me. To be called an author by the likes of Richmond Haskin and treated like a colleague of Flynn McMaster on top of that? Unfathomable.

Just then, Lex appeared in front of me. He'd gone for gray slacks and a navy jacket that brought out his striking blue eyes and impressive biceps. His dark hair was damp and I had to refrain myself from reaching up to run my fingers through it right then and there. Which wasn't a usual impulse when I was in the room with men, but *this* particular man had that kind of effect on me.

He smiled, revealing his even white teeth. "Having fun?"

I turned to make introductions to Richmond, but he was already holding out his hand. "Good to see you again, Detective."

The two of them shook and exchanged pleasantries.

"Any news?" Richmond looked eager.

"Nothing yet," Lex said. "We'll be in touch when we know more."

Richmond nodded. "Any time of day or night, please."

"Of course."

"Off to lunch?" Richmond looked back and forth between us.

"Yes. Would you like to join us?" I was the kind of person who invited everyone to join in, everywhere. I couldn't stand the thought of someone feeling left out of any situation if it seemed like they'd be alone otherwise.

"So kind of you, Lila. Truly. But I've made arrangements with—"

"Richie!" Simone and Selene were suddenly there, dressed exactly alike again. Butter-colored sheaths this time, with chunky gold necklaces. They gave him hugs and fawned over him, practically mewing like kittens who just found a delightful ball of yarn for the first time.

We had *very* different ways of treating our publisher, apparently.

I made introductions all around. The twins, catching sight of Lex, transferred their attention rapidly.

"My, my. You're *yummy*," Selene—according to her name badge—said, narrowing her eyes and looking my boyfriend up and down slowly. I could almost hear a low whistle. "Wow."

"Agreed," Simone added, who had met Lex before many times but never with her sister in tow, which clearly encouraged her to say inappropriate things all the livelong day. She narrowed her eyes, assessing us as a couple. "Aren't *you* lucky, Lila? Considering." She gestured languidly toward me, silently conveying my many shortcomings with a swoop of her slender hand.

There was no universe in which she would resist an opportunity to take a dig. Before I could come up with a fitting retort to her implication that I wasn't in his league, Lex was on it.

"Oh, believe me, *I'm* the lucky one." He grinned at them.

They did not look convinced.

"Shall we go?" Richmond inquired of the twins, offering a bent arm to escort them away. The three of them looked for all the world like an old-timey movie mogul with a starlet on either arm.

We all said goodbye politely.

"Please get me out of here," I said to Lex after they'd turned around. "As quickly as possible."

"With great pleasure," he said.

*   *   *

Later, we were seated in a booth at The Peak House, one of our favorite restaurants. The warm, rustic environment was peaceful, and the company of one person was calming in contrast to the hustle and bustle of the conference.

We'd both ordered Cobb salads and were about halfway through them when Lex put down his fork and smiled at me. "How did your panel go? I'm sorry I couldn't listen. Duty called."

"It was fine. Did you find out anything interesting about Ellis?"

He shook his head and took a sip of iced tea. "No one seems to have had any issues with Ellis Gardner, aside from his having been somewhat of a snob."

"A snob?"

"That's the general consensus. Though I probably shouldn't have mentioned that yet."

I had another bite of Cobb salad while I pondered this. What did *yet* mean? "Is that what his colleagues said, or did that come from other people?"

"People in general." Lex paused. "Before we go any further...I'm in somewhat of a bind here, Lila. I mean, we're doing everything we can to procure the proper information. But I keep getting the sense that we aren't asking the questions we need to ask."

"What do you mean?"

He tapped the table as he thought. "I guess I mean that academic vocabularies and hierarchies are..."

"Baffling?"

"Exactly. Also I get the sense that some things aren't written down anywhere but still kind of matter..."

"You mean they're unstated but understood?"

```

"Yes."

"You've just cracked a most important code, Detective."

"Thank you, Professor." He stretched his hand across the table toward mine. I wove my fingers into his and we sat there for a moment, smiling at each other. Which probably looked ridiculous but it was perfectly fine with me.

Eventually we pulled back so that we could return to our salads.

After a few bites he said, "Anyway, I was wondering..."

"Yes."

Lex raised his eyebrows. "Agreement so soon? I hadn't finished asking my question. What if it was something you didn't want to do?"

I shrugged. "If you're asking, I'm doing."

"What if I'd asked if you would dog-sit while I go on vacation?"

"Glad to."

"Help me paint my front porch?"

"Anytime."

"Darn the holes in my socks?"

"Oh, wait...I guess there *are* limits."

He laughed at that and pushed the oversized bowl away so he could rest his folded arms in front of him. "I may need some help figuring out what happened to Ellis. Given that you've helped us in the past—"

I made a point of gasping and widening my eyes in faux surprise. "Is that an *official* acknowledgment, Detective? I'm shocked. Usually I'm the one having to remind you about my helpful nature."

Lex threw up his hands. "Yes, okay, it's official. It comes from the Chief."

I'd met the jovial Chief Cortez at a holiday fundraiser for the police department. We'd shared a cup of eggnog and a long
```

conversation about the investigations I'd contributed to, unofficially, in the past. It must have made an impact.

"Anyway, I've gotten permission to bring you on as a special consultant." He caught sight of my expression and sighed. "Go ahead. You've earned it. Take a minute to gloat—"

"I'm not gloating. I'm soaking it in." I beamed at him. "You just said that I'm special."

He laughed.

"But seriously, you're asking me to consult? In an *official* capacity?"

"That does seem to be the word of the day. And yes. That's what I'm asking." He leaned forward slightly. "I still wouldn't be able to tell you everything about the case, but I could share more than I normally do. What do you think? Oh, it's pro bono, unfortunately, but you'll have our undying gratitude."

"Are you saying that I don't already have your undying gratitude? Three cases in?" I pretended to pout.

"Let's say that this will cement it." He picked up his glass and held it out so that we could clink our drinks. So we did.

As I took a sip, I heard a loud voice and swiveled my head toward the source.

Dr. Trawley Wellington—chancellor of Stonedale University and owner of the Peak House—was bearing down on us. A tall man with a patrician brow, he could cut an imposing figure when he wanted to do so.

"Dr. Maclean," he boomed. When he arrived at the table, he took note of the empty bowls. "Good to see you enjoying our menu."

His tone somehow had the effect of making me feel as though I hadn't sufficiently conveyed my enjoyment the eight hundred other times I had gone there.

"You remember Detective Archer," I said, nodding to Lex.

"Yes, of course. How are you, Detective?" The chancellor

gave him a tight smile. "Heard about the unpleasantness at Tattered Star Ranch."

Talk about downplaying things.

Lex dipped his chin. "Very unfortunate."

The chancellor turned his attention to me. "How is the conference going? You're on the site committee, correct? I presume you are putting your best foot forward to represent our fine university?"

No pressure. "Doing my best."

"She was just nominated for an award," Lex cut in smoothly, attempting to score me a few points with the most powerful person at the university.

The chancellor blinked without displaying any interest in the details. "Glad to hear that you're doing your part, Dr. Maclean. Keep me posted." He raised his hand in greeting at someone behind us and left abruptly.

Lex and I stared at each other.

"Keep me posted?" I whispered. "What does that even mean?"

He shook his head. "And if he's so interested in how Stonedale University is represented at the conference, why doesn't he attend?"

"Oh, the chancellor is very busy."

"And very important."

"Yes. Very busy *and* very important."

Lex grinned. "Is anyone else from your department going?"

"Calista is coming Saturday. Simone Raleigh is already here, as you saw. But not many other folks study horror or gothic. This conference has a rather narrow focus compared to some of the other ones."

"Like the Modern Language Association one?"

"Well done, Detective."

"I do listen, you know."

I registered a warm little glow inside my chest.

He took a sip of his drink. "Let me ask you this: why do some people stay overnight and others drive in for the day?"

I shrugged. "Personal preference, maybe? Though in this case, it's incredibly expensive to stay there now that they've done the expansion. If I hadn't been comped a room for committee work, I wouldn't be staying there, either."

"I'll have to thank them for that," he said. "I enjoyed falling asleep there with you on my shoulder last night."

"You're welcome to join me again tonight."

He smiled. "Wouldn't miss it."

His phone buzzed and he quickly scanned the text. "Need to get back to the ranch."

"What's the next step? Now that I'm helping with the case and all." I batted my eyelashes at him playfully.

"Right." He grinned. "Let's make a list. Who do you think might have had it out for Ellis?"

"Meredith, Candace, and Richmond all seemed genuinely distraught."

"Who else had contact with him that you know about?"

"Here at the conference? Hanover."

"Already spoke to him," Lex said. "How about not at the conference?"

"Whoever else at the press worked with him. His family. Neighbors and friends. Colleagues at Fairlake University."

"You're doing great."

I thought for a moment. "The scholars who submitted to the critical guide would have interacted with him."

He nodded approvingly. "Good."

"Had you already thought of that?"

"Yes, but keep going."

"Oh, Flynn McMaster was a colleague too."

"So far, we are on the same page. Keep thinking about why

someone could have been angry enough to attack him."

I sighed. "It's so sad. I don't know how you think about these things and not walk around utterly depressed."

Lex met my eyes. "Some days I do. But then I spend an hour with you and it lifts me out of the shadows."

I had just opened my mouth to say something that would have been regrettably gushy when the check was delivered by our hipster waiter with his handlebar mustache.

Saved by the mustache.

Chapter 6

On the way back to the hotel, Lex informed me that he had set up a meeting with all of the contributors to the critical guide immediately following the signing event. We would have the chance to ask questions then. In the meantime, my assignment was to observe the signing, to see if anything looked out of order.

"Out of order?" I touched his arm as he pulled into a parking spot. "What do you mean?"

"Anything that doesn't seem common. You've been to these before, right?"

I picked my bag up from the floor of his Honda as I thought. "I have been to many signings before, yes, but not one that hosted quite so many authors at once. Since this is an anthology—"

"A what?"

"It's another word for collection of texts."

"Got it." He shot me an exasperated look. "So this thing is a critical guide, an anthology, *and* a collection of texts? Why so many words to describe one thing?"

"English teachers like words? I don't know."

He chuckled.

"And yes, Detective, I will perform surveillance and report back. Officially speaking." A bit of glee crept into my voice. "I'm on the case."

He removed the keys and faced me. "Let's get something clear, Lila. This is not an opportunity for you to ramp up into super-sleuth mode or go into overdrive. We don't need you to produce any charts or tables—"

"But you know how much I *like* a good chart. Or table."

"I do. I've seen you in action. Which is why I mention it." He ran a hand through his hair. "We're just interested in any general observations you may be able to provide."

"No super-sleuthing? What's the fun in that? Speaking of which, will I be getting a badge? Something to flash before I launch my probing interrogations?"

"Absolutely not." Lex laughed, then his expression shifted. "And I cannot stress enough the *consulting* part of this arrangement. We are asking you to confer with us. Provide information. Help us think through things. This does *not* give you the right to do anything you wouldn't have done before. You could set some undesirable things in motion."

"What do you mean?"

"Don't go into dangerous situations."

"Even if—"

"Don't pepper people with questions."

"But questions are my—"

"And don't go running in anywhere like some kind of ninja. You are not a member of the police force."

"I didn't know you were all ninjas."

He gave me a look. "I'm serious."

I nodded, trying to appear chastened. "Of course."

"I mean it. I don't want..."

"What? You don't want me to take a chance?"

"No. I don't want anything to happen to you."

Another warm feeling spread throughout my chest. This man literally made me tingle. "Thanks, Lex."

He bobbed his head curtly.

Well, that wouldn't do. I leaned over, preferring to seal our agreement with a kiss.

The signing was set up in the room adjacent to the "Book Lair," which unfortunately meant that it was in the room where Ellis had been found. I wondered whose idea that had been. Not a very good one, in my humble opinion. Not that anyone was asking me.

In the hallway, I paused to send up good thoughts to the recently departed professor, then shivered before going through the door.

The room had been reconfigured. A long line on the left side steered individuals toward the scholars seated at tables at the far end of the room. A cookie and coffee bar had thoughtfully been set up in the middle for those who needed an afternoon sugar boost, and the right side of the room was filled with groups of attendees chatting and partaking of the refreshments. I took a place last in line, training my eyes on the row of anthology contributors, as Lex had asked. Everything seemed to be going smoothly—individuals in line would slide their book across the table to an author, exchange a few words, then the scholar would sign the book and slide it back. The line would move one person to the right, and the whole process would begin again.

As I watched, I heard a familiar voice right behind me. One I didn't particularly care to hear at the moment. Perhaps they wouldn't notice me if I stood very still.

Or did that only work with a T-Rex?

"Are you *sure* you want to be here?" One of the Raleighs asked. "Aside from the obvious...I mean, it's going to take forever."

"Yes," came a swift reply. I didn't recognize the speaker. It was a male voice, though.

"Well, I have half a mind to go right up to the table."

"Please don't do that, Selene."

I silently thanked the man for identifying her.

And for encouraging her to behave like a normal human being.

She sighed. "Why should we have to wait along with everyone else? It's our publisher. Doesn't that give us, like, VIP status or something?"

He laughed. "We're not at a club."

"I know, Becks, but we could be back in our room." Her voice turned cajoling. "We have just enough time. Come on. You know you want to…"

I could feel movement behind me but now I *really* didn't want to turn around. A vigorous smacking suggested that there was a make-out session happening.

"Selene." He cleared his throat. "Stop."

Good for him. It wasn't like we were waiting in line at a carnival ride after kicking back a few brewskis. This was a formal scholarly event, not a date.

Way to draw a boundary, buddy.

I did that thing where you face one way but all of your attention is focused on what's going on behind you. If I were in a Dr. Seuss book, the illustration would have my ears perked up and eyes heading in opposite directions trying to see around myself. Or something like that.

Despite my hyperalert watchfulness, nothing else happened for a moment. She seemed to be following directions and halting her amorous administrations. He wasn't talking.

"Lila!" I cringed that my cover—not very substantial, as it was just comprised of not turning around—had been blown.

Simone stood beside me, presenting the very picture of collegiality. Almost. I knew that beneath those perfect teeth were lies just waiting to be told. Selene slid up next to her sister, and both of them were staring and smiling in an unsettling way at me.

The way two crocodiles might open their jaws and reveal their teeth.

Right before eating you.

"Good afternoon. How are you?" I could be polite with the best of them. My mother had taught me well.

"Congratulations on your nomination," Simone said. Her mother had taught her well too.

It occurred to me that our mothers could have quite the well-mannered rumble if ever brought face to face.

"Congratulations to both of you."

"What a *surprise*," my colleague continued, not sounding at all surprised.

"And an honor." I replied, genuinely feeling that to be the case.

Selene tossed her head. "I don't know how they'll ever choose between us." Her words said one thing, but her head-toss said another.

Simone addressed her sister. "We're in worthy competition, aren't we?"

What was this? I wasn't used to Simone saying anything nice about me.

She directed her gaze to the person standing behind me. "Becks, do you know Lila?"

I spun around to face the previously well-kissed boundary-setter himself, who turned out to be a ruddy-faced preppy, with a flop of blond hair over his brow. I'd seen carbon copies of him at every frat party on film. He grinned and held out his hand. "Beckett Thurber Standhouse."

"The *third*," Selene said loudly, smoothing the hair along her temple. Her large diamond ring seemed familiar somehow.

He grinned at her. "Yes, the third."

"My fiancé," she added.

"That's right," he said.

"We're getting married in August," she informed me. "In the Hamptons."

"Congratulations," I said. "That sounds wonderful."

"It will be. There's been so much planning. Everything has to be perfect. Exquisite. We've been simply drowning in details, haven't we Becks?"

"That we have."

"Though Simone has been a *dream* maid of honor. What a helper." She squeezed the shoulder of her twin, who gave her a big smile, but not before I caught sight of something else on her face. A flicker of exasperation? Hard to tell.

"Anyway, I'm bored now," Selene said abruptly. "Shall we go?"

Beckett studied her face, which now showcased an adorable pout. I saw the future dynamics of his married life stretching out before him and cheered for him to stand strong.

He shrugged. "Of course."

The two of them left holding hands, with Simone trailing slightly behind them. I couldn't imagine what it would be like to be a maid of honor to Selene, who had all the makings of a major bridezilla.

After the signing was over, I filed my first official consultant report.

Which meant I texted Lex that everything had been fine at the signing.

He texted back the number of the small conference room where we would be meeting the contributors and editors. By the time I found the location on the second floor and walked in,

THE SUBJECT OF MALICE 57

everyone was already seated at the large round wooden table. I scurried to the last spot.

"Thank you for bringing us in for this discussion," Candace said warmly. "We're happy to help, however possible."

Lex flipped open the black notepad he used when interviewing witnesses. I'd had it aimed at me a few times in the past. "I'm grateful you all were able to come, and I hope not to take up too much of your time. As you know, we are investigating the death of Dr. Ellis Gardner."

"Are we suspects, Detective?" Richmond folded his hands over his stomach. "I can't imagine why. Ellis was our friend."

Lex maintained his calm demeanor. "I'm just trying to get a sense of the book project that caused such a splash here." He gestured to me. "This is Dr. Lila Maclean—"

"Oh we already know her," Richmond interjected. "She's one of our newest authors. Very pleased to see you, Lila."

I smiled at him as Lex requested that we place our conference badges on the table so that he could record the name of everyone present. He went around the circle, reading the name, glancing at the face, and scribbling in his notepad. We sat silently until one of the men cleared his throat and waved.

"Yes?" Lex looked up.

"Are we going to be here long? I have to meet someone for drinks."

All heads turned toward the detective, who held up one finger while completing his list. "And...done. No, this shouldn't take too long. Why don't we begin with a brief discussion of the project—how it came to be, what happened along the way, etc.?"

Richmond launched forth with a description of how he'd been watching the film adaptation of Flynn's first book and had a powerful eureka moment, realizing that Flynn's work would be the perfect topic for the series concept he'd been toying with. He explained that he'd reached out to Candace and Ellis, English professors at the school, to see if they'd like to join him. The three of them came up with the idea of dividing the book into four parts. The decision to include biography, interviews, and photographs limited the number of critical essays, but it also differentiated the guides from more typical anthologies, which they felt was a positive thing.

He discussed the contributions of those present and gestured to the scholars in turn: Sharita Dawes, an elegant woman with a level gaze, wrote on Bollywood elements; Topher Armitage, a tidy sort with a bright orange bowtie and endearingly crooked grin, wrote on Shakespearean allusions; Lawrence Ling, an athletic man in an oversized hoodie, wrote on video game connections; Winston Hughley, a stout fellow with a long blue pen smudge on his cheek, wrote on comic book influences; and Nan Delancey, a woman with a shock of fuchsia hair that fell over one eye, wrote on representations of the body.

Once their topics had been established, we all looked at Lex, who peered pointedly at me.

Apparently, I was up at bat.

"Aside from working on this collection, do you know each other?" I asked, trying to establish the relationships among participants.

"Only from the email list, right?" Shanita said first. The rest confirmed her statement.

Lex was writing and didn't appear to be waiting to ask another question, so I continued. "How long have you been working on Flynn's books?"

"And movies," Nan murmured, fiddling with one of the safety pins on her shoulder. Her punk-flavored clothing had rows of them in strategic places. She exuded restless energy.

"Yes—thank you. Flynn's books *and* movies."

All of them indicated that it had been the call for papers sent out by Richmond that spurred them to dive in.

"We had an enormous response," Richmond said. "A veritable tidal wave of submissions. People around the world wanted to be part of this project. It took us months to make our way through the abstracts we received and whittle it down. In the end, while competition was vast, your essays prevailed. You should all be very proud of yourselves. Very proud indeed."

"We're grateful, sir," Topher said. The others made sounds of agreement.

"Nothing has been written on McMaster before this," Shanita informed me, smoothing her long dark hair. The gold bracelets on her wrist caught the light.

"Well, that's not exactly true," Winston cut in, his low voice barely audible. He adjusted his tortoiseshell glasses and straightened up in his chair when everyone turned his way. "I mean, he's all over the internet. Lots of people have written about him. And there have been conference presentations."

"Shanita means there is nothing that has been *peer reviewed*," Lawrence said, tapping the table for emphasis.

"True," Winston conceded, his chin lowering slightly.

Lex looked at me questioningly.

"Vetted by other scholars before publication," I explained, "in books or academic journals."

"Peer review can also lead to a request for revisions," Lawrence clarified for Lex. "Or sometimes straight-up rejection. Denial of publication altogether."

"Sometimes? More often than not!" Winston exclaimed. "Peer review can be brutal."

There was a brief period of commiseration with this pronouncement.

Lex made a note.

"Anyway, that's why this critical guide is so important," Nan said. "It will launch discussions of McMaster's work on a new level."

Richmond preened. "We at Fairlake certainly think so."

"And it is well-deserved," Topher said so loudly that his bowtie seemed to quiver. "Flynn's work has captured the minds and hearts of America."

"*That* description may be over the top," Winston ventured, attempting to regain ground after having been corrected earlier, "but he is definitely a success."

"How many films have been made?" Lex glanced around the table.

"Three so far," Nan said, smiling. "A trilogy."

"Three more in production," Winston jumped in. "Which they're calling the *second* trilogy."

"How clever of them," Lawrence said, rolling his eyes.

Winston shot him a look.

Lex went on. "And how many books are out currently?"

"Six," several people said in unison.

"He's working on the seventh," Sharita said. "Set in Tibet."

"Do any of you know him personally?" Lex asked.

The room fell silent.

"I do," Richmond said. "And so do Candace and Ellis..." he stopped, overcome by the mention of his friend.

Candace patted his forearm, and they smiled sadly at each other, then she took out a tissue from her pocket and touched it to her eyes.

Lex shifted slightly in his chair. "Very sorry for your loss." He made eye contact with both professors before continuing. "And how many of the rest of you—aside from Dr. Haskin and Dr. Slaten—knew Dr. Gardner, outside of having worked on this book with him?"

"I met him yesterday," I said quietly.

The detective acknowledged that with a dip of the head. "Anyone else?"

The other scholars remained silent.

Lex flipped the page of his notepad over and waited. My turn again, I guess. I wished he had told me ahead of time to come up with questions so I could be functioning more like a proper investigator, but he hadn't. So I just said the next thing that popped into my head.

"What are your impressions of Flynn, in general, everyone?"

"He's a player," Nan said. "I mean, he's pretty much known for that. Love 'em and leave 'em."

"Known for that?" Winston scowled at her. "What does that even mean? That he dares enjoy the company of women? Is that not allowed in this day and age?"

Sharita spoke gently. "No, that's not what she—"

Winston interrupted, asking Nan to provide evidence for her claims.

"Um, Twitter? There are pictures of him on there with a different woman every week." She leaned back and crossed her arms over her chest. "That *he* posts."

"Maybe they're just friends—" Lawrence began.

"He's not married, is he?" Winston barked. "So what's the problem?"

Nan narrowed her eyes at him. "It's not a problem. It's just a description. Why are you getting so rage-y?"

"I just feel like you wrote him off immediately rather than discussing the importance of his work—"

"I didn't write him off! She asked what our impressions were. I gave mine." Nan made a sound of exasperation. "Give yours, then."

Winston repositioned his glasses and leaned forward. "Flynn is a genius. I don't care what he does in his spare time. *That's* my impression."

Topher waved his hands. "I agree with Winston. Could we please talk about our essays instead?"

That's probably what I should have asked them about in the first place, now that he mentioned it.

I peeked at Richmond and Candace. He was staring sternly at the contributors, as if displeased with the sudden turn of the conversation. Candace had her head tilted away and was still dabbing at her eyes. Seeing their emotion made me want to wrap things up here as soon as possible, so they could have some space to grieve their friend.

Quickly agreeing with Topher, I invited the scholars to describe the focus of their essays. As they went around the table one by one, I noticed that outside of Winston, who pretty much just praised all of the ways Flynn made use of comic conventions, they all put forth arguments that were less celebratory—for example, Sharita focused on cultural appropriation, Nan examined body objectification, Lawrence suggested plot parallels with other texts, and Topher challenged the way Flynn used Shakespearean allusions. It surprised me—given the usual glorification whenever Flynn was mentioned, both in and out of academia, I would have guessed that the earliest scholarship might have matched that.

Eventually, Lex gave me another inquisitive look, which I interpreted to mean that he wanted to wrap things up, and I nodded in agreement.

He thanked everyone for coming and asked for their emails and phone numbers in case he had follow-up questions.

As they all shuffled out, he moved over to my side of the table and sat down heavily.

"Anything of note?"

I pointed out the tone of the scholarship.

He looked thoughtful. "So they didn't just write adoring essays...that's good, right?"

"In terms of scholarship, yes. Absolutely. But..." I couldn't quite articulate fully what I was thinking. It had to do with motive. If there was something significant for us to consider in the approaches of the scholars, I didn't want to miss it. "You know what? I think we should both read the essays tonight. See for sure what we're dealing with."

"Are you giving me homework?" Lex looked pained.

I laughed. "Yes."

"That's the last thing I need right about now," he said, tucking his notepad away in the inside pocket of his blue jacket. "How about you read them and summarize for me?"

I shrugged. "If that's how it has to be."

"You love reading, right?"

"I do love reading."

"And by all accounts, you're quite good at it too. I might even go so far as to call it one of your superpowers."

"I wouldn't call it—"

"So let's put your superpower to good use, Professor."

Flattery will get you, every time.

Chapter 7

Lex went to connect with his colleagues while I made a beeline for the room to take advantage of the small pocket of time before dinner. I had just dropped onto the bed with the critical guide in hand when my phone rang. Glancing at the screen, I smiled and answered.

"I'm *furious* with you..." my mother said loudly.

I braced myself.

"Why didn't you *tell* me you'd been nominated for an award? I've been toasting you with champagne all afternoon and gushing about you to Daphne." There was a swallowing sound. Evidently the champagne was still flowing in New York.

Daphne Duvall was my mother's dearest frenemy. Although they'd been close forever, long before Daphne married a corporate tycoon and my mother became a famous artist known as Violet O, there had always been a fair bit of turmoil in their relationship. That was just how Daphne rolled. But my mother was the type of person who was energized rather than drained by drama, so the friendship served a purpose for her too.

"And then Daphne complained *endlessly* that I didn't tell her first. You know how much she *needs* her gossip."

Daphne wrote a gossip column for a tabloid, so it was literally her job. Between the two of them, my mother and Daphne had quite a pipeline of information coming and going.

"But I'm out of practice telling her things, aren't I, as she hasn't been around for ages, having jetted off to—where was it? Cozumel? Cartagena? Copenhagen? Something with a C, anyway—to be nipped and tucked again, though she told us all that it was for a *spiritual retreat*." She giggled. "She's running out of reasons to give us. I don't know why she won't admit that she's doing *maintenance*. Everyone knows, anyway. No one's eyebrows are *that* high up on their forehead without a little surgical boost. She does look smooth, I'll give her that. But back to *you*, darling, congratulations."

"Thank you. How did you—"

"Calista, of course. If it weren't for her, I wouldn't know *anything* that's happening with my very own daughter."

"We talk all the time, Mom."

"I would not know *one* single thing, Lila. It's tragic. A mother likes to be *in the loop*."

"You are in the loop. And I'll tell you whatever you want to know."

"That's not the point, is it, that you'll tell me something *after* I ask you? I want you to *offer* it. To *want* to tell me."

"I do. It's just very b—"

"Well, do it more often. I know you're busy. But I love you. The loop is *sacred*. Please acknowledge that, darling."

"The loop is sacred. And I love you too."

"Good. Anyway, this afternoon when I was out shopping for a new frock with Daphne—and I did buy a *lovely* purple number for the opening party tomorrow. I know, there's no room for error in that sort of timeline. And I still need shoes. But it's no secret that I like to live on the edge." She laughed. "Poor Daphne couldn't find a *thing*...wait. Where was I going with this? Oh yes! Your cousin texted me the news, so we immediately ran to the most charming wine bar on the block to celebrate. Now, tell me absolutely everything!"

I gave her an overview—excluding the part about Ellis and

the subsequent investigation—and was rewarded with additional kudos and questions, then another round of updates on Daphne's more exasperating behaviors.

"Oh, I've just had the best idea—I should catch the red eye. Wait, *do* you call it a red eye if it goes west instead of east? Maybe not. The point is, I could fly overnight and be there to witness your glorious panel in the morning! I *think* I know where my passport is."

"You don't need your passport to come to Colorado, Mom."

"Are you sure? The rules keep changing. Last time I flew to Paris, I couldn't even bring my *lotion* onboard." An artist of various mediums who was rough on her hands, she made sure a bottle of soothing cream was never far from her at any given time.

"Yes, I'm sure that you don't need a passport. And you are allowed to bring a small container of lotion. Just Google the size."

"Oh, your generation and your Googling. Takes all the *mystery* out of everything. There's something to be said for having to wait longer than four seconds to get an answer, believe me. Back in my day, we suffered for weeks and months at a time, not knowing things. It was almost an *art form*. Wait..." I heard the sound of paper being ripped off of something. "I just had an idea."

I waited for her to jot a note, knowing from experience that she wouldn't be able to hear anything else until she had recorded the concept that would lead to a new project. When I was growing up, she had frequently halted in the middle of grocery shopping, birthday parties, parent-teacher conferences—whatever—to rip a shred of paper from the nearest available source and capture the stirrings of the muse. She'd pull a pencil from somewhere inside her heavy coils of copper hair and scrawl away on something. I'd inherited the tendency to shove writing utensils into my own braid when I was distracted. Sometimes, at the end of the day, there would be a handful in there. It always made me think of her.

I was grateful that she'd taught Calista and me to honor inspiration whenever it occurred. We dropped what we were doing to scribble things down these days too. The lessons of Violet O ran deep.

"Ooh, that's a good one," she murmured.

I took that to mean she was done being inspired for now and we could move on. "Speaking of art, don't you have an opening this weekend? You just mentioned it."

She paused. "Oh, you're right. I don't know what I was thinking. I may have had too much champagne. That's it. I'm cutting myself off." I heard another swallow followed by the clink of glass on granite. "But you know I'd fly to the moon if I could to support you. I'm so proud of you, darling. *Brava!*"

I thanked her and asked her to tell me about her latest work. She enthusiastically complied, and ten minutes later, I felt as though I'd visited the gallery to see her interactive exhibit, "Danger Street." As she described it, the installation featured a tunnel with scenes from noir films silently projected onto the ceiling. Along both walls were red doors in various shapes and sizes. Behind most of the doors were mannequins in gray trench coats onto which a line from a famous mystery was projected. A new door led to a new line from another mystery. Although the quotes had been selected from different books, they wove together into a new layer of narrative. The more doors were opened, the more lines were bestowed, and the further the story progressed. However, behind some of the doors were mirrors, where the line appeared on the viewer as an invitation to reflect upon its relation to their own lives. The deeper the viewer went into the exhibit, however, the darker and foggier it became, until the only thing visible in the final door was not the mannequin or the viewer, but the line itself.

"Do you see? The line is the *end* of the line, darling. But the ending is also the *beginning* of understanding."

My mother had always said things like that.

"It sounds intriguing. Very meta. Congratulations."

"Thank you. I hope it completely *destabilizes* reality for everyone."

My mother had always said things like that too.

There wasn't always an obvious response to be made.

"So many levels of meaning at once...but enough of that. I don't like to explain my art, as you know. Especially if you haven't experienced it yet. Now tell me about Lex. How is he?"

"Great. I've enjoyed helping him with the case—"

"What case?"

I stopped short. I hadn't wanted to mention Ellis. She would worry. Come to think of it, I probably should be worrying too, about being in this hotel with a murderer. If the killer *was* actually staying here. There was no way of knowing. It wasn't like I could simply call the front desk and inquire.

I aimed for intentionally vague. "Oh, a case that required input about academia." There. That should sidestep things nicely.

"It's not another murder, is it?"

I couldn't lie to her. So I explained.

"I'm so sorry to hear that. And I'm glad that Lex is there. Not because you can't take care of yourself—of course you can. You're a strong woman. But because having a person who is skilled in weaponry nearby makes me feel better."

"Skilled in weaponry?" Did she think I was dating a medieval knight?

"You know what I mean. Someone with firepower."

We did another round of well-wishing about our prospective activities and were just saying goodbye when she launched her final piece of advice.

"Please be careful, darling. You never know who is lurking outside your hotel room door."

Great. Now I would be thinking about *that* all weekend.

Chapter 8

I stared into the shallow hotel closet with dismay, realizing that I hadn't packed clothing that could be considered "Western wear." Primarily because I didn't own any. Having lived out here a few years, it was high time to invest in boots at the very least, and I'd intended to shop for this event. For now, I'd just have to be dressed as a professor who likes the theme but didn't make it all the way to the end of her pre-conference to-do list.

Thus resolved, I set off for the evening's events. I was early, but it was lovely to go outside, where it was cooler. I'd attended far too many conferences where everything took place indoors, and we all emerged at the end of the weekend pale and blinking, shrinking back like vampires at the unfamiliar sunlight after several days of recycled air and nonstop Muzak.

Wandering down the twisting stone path, I admired the effect of the time-smoothed gray stones. Now that I was officially—I smiled at the thought—helping Lex with the case, I felt inspired to make the most of my seating arrangement and gather information. However, we'd already spoken with the scholars, and Lex hadn't given me any additional direction. I didn't even know who was first and foremost on the suspect list.

I'd just have to aim for anyone who might have known Ellis in any capacity whatsoever.

At that moment, someone called my name, and I turned to see my cousin scurrying down the path, the red scarf she had artfully thrown over her blue denim dress swinging out behind her. I complimented the star embroidery that added some Western flair and gave her a quick hug. Her green tea scent, something she'd loved since high school, surrounded me. She'd recently let her usual platinum bob grow out, and for tonight, she'd pulled back her hair into a ponytail that showed off turquoise earrings hanging almost to her shoulders.

"I thought you weren't coming until tomorrow, Cal?"

She smiled and gave my arm a squeeze. "After our phone call, I changed things up."

"Cousin to the rescue." I smiled affectionately at her. "Did you get your book done?"

"Like a boss."

"Good for you."

"Technically, anyway. I'll finish up on Sunday when I get home. This is more important."

"You are so sweet."

"I'm not about to let the Raleighs ruin—"

"Ruin what?" Simone appeared out of nowhere. "What was that you were saying, Calista?"

"You heard me, Simone." The two faced off—Simone was taller, and her elegant olive suit with black trim lent her an air of authority, but my petite cousin bristled with energy. "I said: I am not about to let the Raleighs ruin everything."

"I have no idea what you're talking about." Simone's tone was icy.

A slow smile spread across Calista's face. "That's what you're going with? You have no idea what I'm talking about? All right. How about this, Simone? *You will*, soon enough."

Simone's mouth fell open. She attempted—but failed—to pull off a casual shrug before stalking away. It came across more like an angry twitch.

Calista grinned at me, her gray eyes sparkling. "How fun."

"What did you mean by that?"

"Nothing. I just wanted to unsettle her a little." She winked.

"Well, it worked. I don't think I've ever seen her speechless before."

"I'll take that as a win."

"You know you're going to pay for that," I said, half-joking. I'd certainly experienced the wrath of Simone in the past.

"Bring it on. I'm not afraid of her."

"Of course you're not. Though you're going to have to face her at school. We're colleagues." This wasn't coming out right, but I was feeling protective. I didn't want Simone to set her sights on Calista.

"It wasn't very collegial of me, it's true. But she hasn't been acting very collegial to you." Calista looped her arm into mine and pulled me forward. "Don't worry about it, Lil. Let's go find some excellent seats. I didn't pull out my fanciest denim for nothing."

We entered the barn, which looked exactly like it had the previous evening, except that there was a slideshow rotating through Flynn McMaster's book covers on a large screen set up on the stage. A song from the first film adaptation was blaring through the speakers—swelling, sweeping, adventurous music. The kind that made you imagine jumping onto a table and unsheathing a sword.

Good thing we didn't have a sword right now. I might have been tempted to point it at the twins.

Calista made her way to the centermost table at the front and set her scarf over one of the chairs facing the stage. She patted the one next to it. "Sit here and I'll go rustle up some drinks."

I did as she said. It had been a long day and I was glad to have a moment to read through the emails that had flowed in from students and colleagues. Our teaching and service responsibilities didn't stop while we were at a conference fulfilling our professional development obligations. Scrolling through messages on my phone, I could sense the room filling up around me, but I remained focused on the screen.

Until someone plunked down beside me and made a declaration.

"My kingdom for a beer!" Nate Clayton smiled at me, his brown hair tousled as usual and his blue eyes crinkled up rather adorably. Like they did.

I squeaked in surprise. "What are you doing here?"

"Calista told me what's going on. I thought you might want some additional company."

Nate was one of the first faculty members at Stonedale to befriend me; his office was next to mine, and we both taught American Literature. He'd quickly become one of my favorite people there. "Thank you so much."

"Tweren't nothing, ma'am," he said, tipping an imaginary hat. "She saw online that some friends had posted about not being able to make it to the conference, so we wrangled their rooms at a very discounted fee. And of course the conference chair was happy to take more of our money for this here swanky dinner."

"I'm sorry—I'll pay you both back."

"Nothing doing. Truth be told, when I heard it was Flynn McMaster giving the keynote, there was even more of an incentive to show up." He leaned an elbow on the table. "We went to grad school together, don't you know."

"You did?" I stared at him. "You never mentioned that."

"Well, it's not like we walk around listing our rosters of grad school classmates on the regular."

"Good point. It's just he's—"

"So famous. Though I never would have guessed it in grad school. Didn't figure him for an action hero guy. Then again it was during our master's. Things could have changed when he was working on his doctorate."

"How well do you know him?"

"Very well," he said. "Despite totally misreading his interest in genre fiction. To be fair to myself, though, he kept that quiet."

"Maybe he was worried that he wouldn't be taken seriously or something. You know, because he wasn't writing literary fiction."

"He wasn't writing any kind of fiction, as far as I knew. But yes, what you said. Academia can be snobby about that sort of thing. As you know."

"Unfortunately." I'd gone three rounds and then some regarding the "significance" of the mystery course I taught. There was disagreement in some circles about the "place" of popular fiction in the study of literature. And I still wasn't sure it wasn't going to come back and cause an issue when I was up for promotion. But that fight was for another day. "What's Flynn like?"

Nate twisted his lips. "Funny, brilliant, and as much as it pains me to admit this given that he's incredibly successful and I'm not at all successful—"

"You are successful," I insisted.

"Hardly. I'm just a dude who works around the clock on a subject very few people care about—"

"I do."

"Aside from you, I mean. But most people aren't holding their breath to hear my thoughts on Nathaniel Hawthorne."

"Wait a minute there, dude. What about all the Hawthorne scholars? And the Romantic scholars? And the Gothic scholars? And so on and so forth. There are plenty of us holding our breath to hear what you think. Start sharing, please."

"That helps, actually." He winked at me. "But when I'm not working on that, I'm grading papers—for a pittance, I might add—plus, as my mother constantly reminds me, I'm still depressingly single."

"What about Amanda?"

"We broke up."

"Oh no. What happened?"

Nate leaned back and crossed his arms. "She dumped me."

"I'm sorry. Are you okay?"

He shrugged. "Getting there."

"If you need anything—"

"I know. Thanks, Lila."

An awkward pause happened—as it always did when we came close to discussing any romantic matters, given that we'd shared a pretty powerful kiss once. It shouldn't have hung over our relationship the way it did, but we hadn't talked about it right away. Then the more time went by, the harder it seemed to be to talk about it. So we just pretended it hadn't happened and that there wasn't anything lingering between us. Though I think we both suspected that there was.

Nate cleared his throat. "But back to Flynn..."

Thank goodness.

"...he was also cool, you know? Enough of a rebel that people admired him for speaking out, but not so rebellious that he got kicked out. The women went wild for him." He rolled his eyes. "Though he didn't have that man bun in grad school. That's new."

"Are you not a fan of the man bun?"

He squinted at the stage. "Jury's still out. But I'll say this: it appears to be working for him."

"Not exactly answering the question."

"Style is a personal thing."

"Amen to that." I gestured down to my own clothes, which were all black—as usual. It wasn't that I didn't like other colors. It was just that I liked them better on other people.

"It suits you," he said simply. "And then there's..." he waved over his own rumpled blue button-down shirt and cargo pants that he favored.

"Suits you too."

We smiled at each other. While there indeed were plenty of plaid shirts and Stetsons surrounding us, properly following the conference guidelines, at least we were breaking the rules together. Or so I thought.

"In honor of the theme, I did do this—" he pulled his legs out from under the table to reveal a handsome pair of brown cowboy boots.

"I was just thinking about boots before dinner."

"What a strange thing to ponder."

I laughed. "I mean, I was wondering if it was time to acquire some. This dress code has revealed some potential shortcomings of my closet. Are those new?"

"Nope." He wiggled one foot back and forth. "Very old."

"I've never seen them before."

"You don't know *everything* about me, Lila Maclean."

I studied them for a minute. "Are those from when you lived in Kansas?"

His shoulders slumped. "Maybe you *do* know everything about me."

"They're very nice, in any case."

"You know, I forgot how they make me feel. When I walk it probably looks like I'm spoilin' for a fight." He held his arms slightly away from his body but curved in, like a weightlifter. "Mighty."

I laughed. "Be careful with your mighty shoes, then."

"They're *boots*," he said, shaking his head. "Not shoes. Mighty boots. Don't mess with my swagger."

Calista appeared, juggling drinks. She handed Nate a beer, then sat down on the other side of me and passed me a glass of cabernet with lots of ice. Or as I referred to it, "a wine slushie."

I pointed at Nate's bottle of Peak House Ale, the brand that the chancellor had decided to make available outside of the brewpub, which had turned out to be quite profitable in our little college town. "How did you know he wanted a beer?"

"When *don't* I want a beer, is the real question," he said, regarding the bottle fondly.

"Aside from that, I acquired knowledge through the magic of texting." Calista laughed. "I took his order."

"You're so thoughtful." Nate said to her.

She dipped her head, accepting his praise. "I try."

"Anyone else coming?" I hoped her boyfriend Francisco and my next-door neighbor Tad, more of our merry band of department thirty-somethings, might make it, though I didn't anticipate their attendance since the conference topic didn't address either of their specialties.

"No," Calista said, taking a small sip of her white wine before setting it down on the snowy tablecloth. "Fran's at a conference in California, and Tad is up in Aspen with Luke for a getaway weekend. It's just the three of us. And these fine folks," she indicated the rest of our table. Every seat had been taken. I'd been so focused on the conversation that I didn't even notice other attendees had arrived.

We all leaned back as the servers set down small plates with our salad course: spiky leaves festooned with colorful shreds of unidentifiable vegetables. A swirl of something purple had been squirted along the rim—presumably the dressing. I poked gently with my fork at the concoction, hoping to locate some regular old iceberg lurking underneath. Fancy salads tend to throw me off—I wasn't fond of any lettuce that had a tail.

"I'm so excited to hear the keynote," said the woman seated next to Nate. Her silver bolo tie clasp was shaped like a turtle. "I can't believe Flynn McMaster is here."

The table broke out into praise for his books, then slid into fervent debate about which of the films was the best and why. Evidence was offered for all options, but the table remained in a draw, largely because of a difference of opinion about casting. The actor chosen to play Dr. Powell Block—a brilliant professor well-versed in gothic literature whose quest was always to prove that the monsters depicted in such tales were real and that humans needed saving from them—was Tristan Oldsmith, a British dreamboat prone to ripping off his shirt to show his washboard stomach at the slightest provocation.

Some felt that Tristan was not serious enough to pull off the character they'd been imagining through their series reading.

Others saw Tristan as the perfect blend of brain and brawn.

I agreed with the latter group. I wouldn't object to spending two-plus hours watching Tristan Oldsmith do *anything*. He had charisma to spare.

After we'd been served a slice of apple pie with a toothpick flag featuring tiny boots with spurs, Acadia Branson took the stage. Gone was the tailored suit of yesterday—instead, she had a plaid shirt beneath a fringed vest with a sheriff's star attached, and a pair of jeans with boots. She made some announcements, including a reminder about the square dance and horse show following dinner, then switched smoothly into an introduction that listed all of Flynn's achievements. She went through his scholarly accomplishments, for which the crowd clapped politely, but as she began a glowing description of the Powell Block series, the anticipation rose. The audience applauded and whistled at the mention of each title of the books and films: *The Cave of the Sibyl, The Spell of the Sorcerer, The Key of the Ghostworld, The Lair of the Vampire, The Realm of the Undead,* and *The Crypt of the Creeper.* Conference audiences are usually gracious, but this kind of adulation was like nothing I'd ever experienced before at any academic event. When she reached the end of her remarks and asked us to welcome Flynn McMaster, the lights went out. Gasps were audible, and, for one excruciating moment, no one moved.

The theme music for the films began—its jaunty, operatic sound filling the room—and spotlights swirled over the crowd as though we were at a movie premiere. The screen switched from the flow of covers to a clip from the first movie. As Powell Block exchanged his famously witty banter with the Sybil, the audience said the words along with him. The clip ended abruptly, and the room went dark again. When the spotlight came back up, Flynn McMaster was at the podium, wearing another flowing white shirt over dark pants. His hair was pulled back, emphasizing his high cheekbones, and an array of necklaces and bracelets were visible.

"Quite the entrance," Nate said to me, under the cover of applause. "That's so Mac."

Flynn held up his hands, acknowledging the adoration, then pressed his palms downward against the air, silently requesting a reduction in volume. Once things had subsided, he leaned into the microphone. "Thank you for your warm welcome. And thank you," he turned to Acadia, standing on the opposite side of the stage, "for that introduction. Surely much better than I deserved, but I'll take it."

Laughs rippled through the room. Probably anything he said was going to hit the bullseye.

"I've been asked to talk about my work, which I will, but I hope you'll indulge me first upfront. I've got something important to say. After all, it's not often that before he gives a keynote, an author is presented with a critical guide, purporting to explain his work." Flynn paused, looking up at the ceiling. "Reading through that was a remarkable experience. Especially since..." He levelled his gaze at the crowd. "They got it so *wrong*."

Nate chuckled, obviously expecting Flynn to deliver a punchline that would negate the bitterness of what he'd just said. But Calista gripped my forearm as shock waves rippled through the room. Then the audience began to buzz. I could hear snippets of what was being said all around me.

"Did he just say—"

"You've got to be kidding—"

"This is going to be good—"

"Talk about egotistical—"

Authors didn't usually address material written by scholars; most of them didn't even respond to reviews—or at least they were expected *not* to do so. This was something altogether different: a direct confrontation of essays that could actually help his career if they were well-received. It didn't make sense that he would speak out against them.

Flynn wiggled the microphone, causing a shriek that immediately silenced the conversations. "I wish I were joking. I do know it's an honor to be the subject of the first book in this series, and I am extremely grateful to Fairlake University Press for choosing my novels and films to focus on. And what I have to say is all the more delicate since it is my own institution that published it. I don't want there to be any tension with colleagues, but I must speak out."

Acadia took two steps forward, then shielded her eyes with a hand over her brow as she scanned the audience. She was clearly looking for someone, though I didn't know whom one might call for help in the case of Keynote Speaker Gone Rogue.

Flynn continued. "Let's be brutally honest, shall we? That's something you don't always find in academia." He paused, as if to allow laughter, which didn't come.

I guess he *could* miss the bullseye after all.

He stepped out from behind the podium, holding the microphone with both hands and peering earnestly at the crowd. "Look, I'm an English professor. I know how important it is to publish your scholarship. Your very career depends on it. But my vantage point has changed. And I do want people to write about my books—don't get me wrong. It's just that I want them to talk about my work *properly*."

The audience responded audibly—a mixture of gasps and comments. The room filled with palpable indignation.

"Are you saying your work is too complicated for us to understand?" A disgruntled voice—presumably professorial—piped up behind us.

Flynn paused. "No. I'm speaking more precisely about drawing a line."

"Annnnnnd..." The voice pushed back, drenched in sarcasm.

"I'm comparing you to anyone who comes into my fictional world."

"Now *I'm* in your scenario?" The voice screeched a little in its outrage.

"If you so choose."

There was a snort behind us.

The author blinked. "Do you understand?"

"No," said the voice angrily. "Enlighten us."

A man on the other side of the room began waving his arms madly.

Flynn caught sight of him. "Oh, I know. Once the book is published, it doesn't belong to me anymore. I'll allow that. But"—he produced a winning smile—"I do feel compelled to insist that I *was* trying to say something and I'd just like to be heard. Correctly."

The audience murmured amongst themselves again.

"Is this really such a stretch? Think of it this way: If

someone built a car that was green and everyone claimed it was red, wouldn't that be incorrect?" Flynn began to pace. "Who am I if I don't stand up for my own work? Don't you stand up for what you've created?"

People began nodding their heads.

He stopped walking and faced the crowd. "Haven't *you* ever been misunderstood?"

A smattering of applause broke out.

"So when does the time come to take a stand? Say no?"

He let the words sink in.

The clapping grew louder.

"Let us *all* resist. Let us say no. No, no, no!"

The applause was thunderous.

He switched the microphone to the other hand. "I *will* say that the essays in this book were technically strong—even fascinating. I enjoyed reading them all, and if it were not focused on my own work, I would probably have closed the cover and went on about my day feeling satisfied. But they absolutely missed—every single one—what I was *trying* to do as an *artist*. I had a *point*. And I wouldn't continue to work as hard as I do, every day, to create stories for you, if there wasn't one. This is about you too."

Someone yelled out, "We love you, Flynn!"

He bowed his head. "Thank you. My readers are the most important thing to me. I don't want to let a single one of you down." Flynn whipped the microphone out into the air and swirled it around like a lasso. The crowd gasped. He pulled the mic in closely again under his chin and tilted his head sideways. "I invite you to join me. C'mon. Right now. Say no!" He held the microphone out toward the crowd, who yelled "NO!"

"And again."

"NO!"

Flynn nodded approvingly. "Good. Now you know you can

do it. Give yourselves a round of applause."

Nate, Calista, and I exchanged glances. This was the strangest keynote ever.

Robust applause continued until he raised his hands over his head. After the crowd had quieted, he smiled again. "Thank you. You have just inspired me to announce that I'm going to take another stand."

The audience fell silent.

"I will leave academia at the end of the semester in order to pursue my writing full-time."

He didn't actually do a mic drop, but it was as if he had.

There was a deafening roar this time.

He'd managed to turn things around.

I revised that thought as the sound of chairs scraping the floor in the back of the room drew my attention. I spun to see all of the scholars Lex and I had interviewed earlier leaving together. They went through the double doors at the front of the barn, which slammed shut.

I didn't blame them one bit.

As I twisted back, I caught sight of Richmond, two tables over, sitting rigidly, his hand over his mouth. Candace, next to him, was rubbing her forehead wearily. Meredith and Hanover were both staring at Flynn like they'd never seen him before, obviously shocked at what he'd said.

Flynn walked back behind the podium. "This may be the only chance I have to correct the record. I hope that by being honest, I've inspired you to look at the things in your life or career that aren't working and to take your own kind of stand." He looked into the wings and nodded. "Before I go on, I've got a little gift for you."

A woman with wispy brown hair emerged, a stack of paper in her arms. She made her way down the stairs on the side and began distributing pages to the closest table.

"I'm so grateful for your enthusiasm for my books and the films. Thank you for your support. My publisher has given me special coupons for you conference attendees—40 percent off of your next purchase of a Powell Block book. Also, there's a code you can enter online to receive two free tickets to the forthcoming film."

He got the *most* applause for that.

Chapter 9

Flynn went on to show us the trailer for the fourth film in the series—also known as the "first in the second trilogy"—due out next year. We were, he told us, the first to lay eyes on it anywhere. That earned him even more points back from the crowd.

Then he told us some behind-the-scenes anecdotes that had people laughing so hard they were wiping tears away. All seemed to be forgiven by most.

His charm was undeniable.

His storytelling ability was admirable.

His attack on my publisher, however, had been terrible.

When the lights came up, I went over to where Richmond and Candace remained. Meredith and Hanover were nowhere to be seen.

Richmond was staring at his empty water glass.

"I'm so sorry—" I began.

"Nothing to be said about it. Nothing at all," Richmond said, shifting his eyes to me. "He took us down. He did. We'll just have to fight our way back up."

Candace had turned sideways in her seat and was watching him intently. "We'll figure something out," she said consolingly to Richmond. "Don't worry."

"Oh!" He turned to her in surprise. "But we're *already* on it, Candace. That's where Meredith and Hanover have gone. Back to their rooms to make necessary calls. Sound the alarm. Rally the troops. In fact, we should go join them."

"Do you need any help? If there's anything I can—"

"Thank you, Lila. We'll let you know." Clearly, he wasn't in the mood for consolation. He lifted his chin, straightened his tie, and pushed back his chair. When Candace followed suit, he offered her his arm and she took it. They moved away and were quickly swallowed up by the crowd.

"Well, that was something else," Calista said, appearing at my elbow.

Nate shook his head. "He turned that keynote speech into...I don't even know what to call it. A self-help seminar with bonus movie clips?"

"It was like a cult meeting." Calista's expression was thoughtful. "Do you think Flynn was under the influence of something? That might explain a few things. I mean, who does he think he *is* to tell everyone they're reading his books wrong?"

"He might have just been high on fame. But more importantly, how are you feeling, Lila?" Nate searched my face for an indication.

"I don't know. There's a little embarrassment that my publisher has been shamed, maybe, mixed in with some pretty strong curiosity about what the essays said that Flynn found so offensive."

"Maybe we should ask him directly?" Calista tipped her head toward the stage.

"Did he put his complaints on the flyer?" I glanced at their hands, which were empty. "That sure would make everything easier."

"I don't think so, but she didn't come to our table yet." Nate craned his neck to find her. "She's right there. Hi there!" He waved.

The woman handing out coupons broke away from Acadia, who appeared to be livid, and sidled over. "Thank you. I was getting chewed out."

"Why?" Calista widened her eyes.

"She thinks I should have refused to help him after what he said up there. He ruined her keynote, she said. I get where she's coming from, but what am I supposed to do? They told me to hand these out." She held up a few pieces of paper. "Please take the last of them?"

"Definitely. We'll take them off your hands." Nate seized the flyers and passed them around.

She rolled her shoulders in relief. "Thank you. By the way, because you saved me, you get an invite to Flynn's after-party. Free drinks. Interested? If anyone gives you a hard time at the door, tell them Acadia sent you."

"Yes," I said firmly before my friends could decline. I wanted to talk to Flynn, see what his relationship with Ellis was like. "Thank you for the invitation..." I squinted at her nametag. "Tanya."

"Sure thing. Room 1020, the VIP floor. Party starts after the rodeo," she said over her shoulder as she walked away.

"Wait, we're going to a rodeo?" Nate asked, delighted.

"When in rodeo-land..." Calista replied.

"But first, there's the square dance," I reminded them. The wall that divided the ballroom from the other half of the event hall had been pushed back, and people were streaming over.

As we moved along with the crowd, a spritely gentleman with a long white beard took over the microphone and urged us to form groups of eight. The sound of bows rasping across strings, releasing tiny bursts of musical notes, came from the stage. While the bearded man introduced himself as our caller,

Howard, we joined a group in the middle of the room. Without any discussion about it, Nate and I slid into one side of the square. Calista and a handsome bald professor who asked if she'd like to partner up were opposite us. To our left and right were couples I didn't recognize.

Howard walked us through a number of the terms he'd be using—specifying how to perform steps like do-si-do and allemande left—before the band started up for real. We bowed to our partners, to the corners, and the dancing began. While promenading, I caught sight of Selene along the far wall, racing up to Beckett and throwing herself into his arms. They appeared to be picking up where they left off at the book signing.

I turned my attention back to the square dance. It wasn't hard to follow the calls, but it moved quickly. After a few minutes, I had relaxed enough to enjoy it, aside from the very sweaty palms of one of my square-mates. During another promenade, I saw Simone walk up to her sister and pull her out of Beckett's arms. I hoped she was giving her some sisterly advice on the inadvisability of Extreme PDA. But whatever they were talking about, it didn't seem to be friendly. They were yelling right in each other's faces.

If only the music wasn't so loud, maybe I could hear what they were on about.

Then again, we were here to dance, not eavesdrop.

A few songs later, Howard told us that the tip was over and we'd be taking a short break. When we returned, he advised us we should form new groups of eight, mix things up.

We said thanks all around our square and drifted over near the door to take advantage of the cool breeze.

"Don't know about you, but I am definitely ready for a break," Nate said, wiping his forehead with his palm.

"I could leave," Calista said. "How about you, Lila?"

"Sure. Rodeo time?"

"I've never been to a rodeo," Calista said. "Though I *have* been to the rodeo museum in Colorado Springs."

"Giddy up," Nate said.

"Actually," Calista corrected him, "I think 'cowboy up' is proper rodeo parlance. Though I may be remembering that wrong."

"With all due respect," Nate replied, "I'll never give up my giddy up. Now let's go find them horsies."

The so-called "rodeo" was more like a short display of horse tricks. After we'd watched them jump and parade in a circle while we listened to some professors behind us argue about the welfare of animals involved in rodeos, we returned to the main hotel, a rather dejected trio.

"That wasn't as fun as I thought it would be." Nate punched the elevator button.

"Let's not talk about it," Calista said. "Instead, let's focus on what happened at dinner. Why do you think Flynn did that? I feel for the scholars who wrote those essays."

"I do too." I pulled my jacket closed. It had gotten cold after the sun went down.

"Also for you, of course, Lil. Since it's your publisher."

"Thanks."

"No one wants to be associated with a publisher that gets bad press," Nate said.

"She knows that," Calista snapped.

He looked hurt for an instant but shook it off, like a puppy who just got in trouble for shredding the newspaper.

"Sorry," my cousin said to him. "I didn't mean to lash out. It just made me furious that Flynn went off and Lila's caught up in it."

"I appreciate both of you," I said. "Please know, however,

that I am not going to worry about someone rejecting me because my book came out from the press that Flynn McMaster slammed. Not for a single second."

"Boom! There you go." Nate high-fived me.

"But I do feel bad for them. Why would he do that when they were so excited about *him*? Also, the editors were his colleagues at the university."

"He must have known he was going to quit or he wouldn't have even tried it," Nate said. "He wouldn't want to face them at another faculty meeting after humiliating them."

"Perish the thought," I said.

"He could have been trying to get attention," Calista mused. "For sales?"

"You mean the no-publicity-is-bad-publicity idea?" I thought for a moment. "Doesn't it seem obvious that bad publicity *is* bad publicity, though?" Oh no. Maybe Chancellor Wellington's endless quest for good publicity was rubbing off on me.

Nate agreed. "And does Flynn really *need* more attention? That dude is everywhere right now. If not his books, then his films. If not his films, then the author himself doing interviews and whatnot."

"You know, there is one thing we haven't considered..."

They both stared at me.

"Couldn't it have been just what Flynn said? I mean, I don't know him at all, but is it possible he was simply being honest about how he felt? He thinks the scholars missed the point? Misread his work?"

Nate considered this. "He is a pretty straight shooter. Known in grad school for standing up for things he believed in. Professors even sometimes complained about the way he would get up on a soapbox."

We stared at him this time.

"Well, they didn't complain to his face," Nate said. "I overheard some of the faculty in the copy room once. They felt that Flynn would try to cut them down to size about something they'd spent a lot of energy and time teaching. It was taken as a challenge to their authority."

"I can understand why that would be annoying," Calista nodded. "But were the things he took a stand on sensible? In other words, was Flynn simply trying to be a thorn in their sides, or did he really believe the things he said?"

"He really believed them." Nate tapped a finger on his lips. It was distractingly cute. "I think, anyway."

"But in this case, even if Flynn believes what he's saying, he can't stop scholars from writing whatever they want to write about his books. He doesn't get to control how the books are interpreted. And as a professor, he knows that. So he actually has nothing to gain, does he?" I couldn't make any sense of it.

"Except perhaps feeding his ego," Calista mused. She turned to Nate. "Does he have a big ego?"

"Flynn always had a healthy ego. But the film deals may have kicked it up to the next level." He paused as the doors opened with a ding.

We found ourselves face to face with the Raleighs and Beckett Standhouse. For a second, no one moved, then Nate and Beckett burst into hearty greetings and did one of those bear hugs with much back slapping. They'd gone to graduate school together too, I realized in the midst of their exclamations.

Somewhere in there, Nate invited them to come with us to the after-party. Simone and Selene both lit up at the invitation, and it became clear that we'd all be attending, so we rode together up to the tenth floor, where the VIP suites were located. Calista and Simone gave each other the side-eye the whole time. I smiled politely at the twins and pulled out my phone, then sent a message to Lex about Flynn McMaster's after-party.

He texted back: *You managed to get invited to the man of the hour's party? You never cease to amaze me, Professor.*

Ditto, I typed. *Join us if you can.*

Music was blaring, ricocheting off of the walls as we made our way to Flynn's suite at the end of the hallway. The main area boasted a kitchen with marble island and high-end gadgetry next to a black lacquer dining table with twelve red leather chairs. Straight ahead, a wide balcony was visible through an open sliding glass door—in the moonlight, you could just barely make out the mountain tops. The town of Stonedale lay between here and there, creating rows of twinkling lights in the darkness.

On the other side of the room, a stone fireplace held court with three blue curved leather sofas and a massive round ottoman in the center. Every space was taken up by people talking and laughing, drinks in hand. Corridors shot off in both directions from the main room, heading presumably to sleeping areas and bathrooms. Or maybe to a chamber full of wizards or a stall where the unicorns lived. I actually had no idea what one might find in a VIP suite.

Flynn uncurled himself from the ottoman and ambled over to where we were clumped in the doorway. He gave both Beckett and Nate a hearty slap on the back. There were more hugs and exclamations. Then Flynn stopped short and stared at Simone and Selene.

"Oh," he said, his voice dropping a notch. "Come in, please." He'd transformed from frat boy to elegant bachelor without missing a beat. After they'd talked for a bit, he turned his attention to Calista and me. We introduced ourselves and said that it was very nice to meet him. He said the same. We were steered toward the dining table, which held a variety of drink fixings and finger foods. Everyone loaded up with refreshments of their choice and moved into the fireplace area. By some miracle, the majority of previous occupants had decided to go outside and stare at the night sky, so there was space for all of us.

Flynn was again on the ottoman, positioned in front of the curved sofa section on the right, chatting mostly with Beckett and Nate. The Raleighs were on the middle section, and my cousin and I took the left. Suited me fine. I could hear everything but didn't feel pressured to talk.

I was biting into a veggie eggroll when I was almost blinded by the dazzle of Selene's ring. Calista elbowed me and nodded that way, raising her eyebrows.

"They're engaged," I said.

"Who's they?"

I mumbled, trying to be quiet. "Beckett and Selene."

"Who?"

"Beckett and Selene," said the woman herself, enunciating while dangling her hand in front of Calista. "Me. I'm Selene."

"Sorry," I said.

"Oh, no problem. We Raleighs have incredibly good hearing, among other things." Of course they did.

I introduced Calista to Selene, officially. We'd ridden in the elevator together, but Nate and Beckett had been enthusiastically filling each other in on the happenings of their classmates since graduation, so there hadn't been any additional conversation.

Simone looked over, pressing her lips together at the sight of her sister and my cousin talking.

Now it was my turn to elbow Calista. She followed my gaze and reached across Selene's lap to touch Simone lightly on the wrist. "I'm sorry about before," she said simply.

Simone studied her face as if expecting something else to follow but ultimately judging Calista to be sincere. She nodded once and said, "Thank you. And I'm sorry for just walking off like that."

My mouth fell open. Never in my long history with Simone Raleigh had I ever received any sort of apology for her many trickeries.

Not that I could remember, anyway.

And even if I had received one, it most certainly had not been a real one.

Maybe Simone had thought about it and realized that it wasn't politically smart of her to have any issue with a tenured professor. In which case, she would be right.

"'Scuse me," a man with a crooked hat said, slurring slightly. "I'm cold." He pointed toward the fireplace, and we all slid backwards to make room for him as he teetered delicately forward. When he had almost passed us, he tripped, waving his arms to regain his balance and throwing the dark brown contents of his glass into the air.

Most of it landed on Selene and Simone, who shrieked and leapt up. The man reached out to sop up the spill on the laps of the twins, who shrieked again and stepped out of his grasp.

"Don't *grope* us," Selene admonished him loudly. "You've already ruined our vintage Chanel."

Flynn hustled the man off into the kitchen and returned with towels and a bottle of club soda and salt that he handed to the Raleighs. Several minutes passed while they attended to the dark stains. A profuse apology was made and accepted, though without much enthusiasm. Eventually, the twins were resettled on the sofa, mouths set in grim lines.

"Are you okay?" Flynn asked. "Very sorry about that, again."

"It's not your fault," Simone said, softly.

"But tell your friend that it's going to cost *scads* to clean these properly." Selene said nastily, her eyes glittering.

"Please." Her sister's cheeks were flushed. "Let it go."

"Fine. We'll pay for it ourselves." Selene drew herself up. "Fortunately, we can afford it."

Well, that was a rather gauche comment. Even I knew that, and I had never taken etiquette lessons.

An awkward silence hovered over the room.

"Your ring is gorgeous," Calista said brightly to Selene, attempting to distract her. "May I look at it more closely?"

Selene swayed her hand carelessly in front of us. I leaned in. The immense stone was cut in an unusual shape—like a snowflake, with six points jutting out from the center. Many carats were sitting on a thick gold band, with engraved swirls cascading down both sides.

"Stunning," I murmured. "This may sound strange, but I feel like I've seen that exact ring before. Might I have seen it in a magazine?"

Selene laughed. "Hardly."

"Is it a popular cut?"

She snatched her hand away and shook her head. "No, in fact, it's a very rare cut. It was created especially for Beckett's family. It's been handed down for several generations from one bride to the other. Right, Simone?"

Simone shifted her eyes toward the ring and dipped her head in agreement.

Selene preened. "It's ridiculously valuable. His grandmother was the last to wear it as a wedded woman. The Standhouses said they're happy that someone in the family is getting married, so it doesn't sit in a box. And you should see the diamond band that goes with it. To die for."

"Does it come with its own security guard?" I joked.

"No," Selene took my question seriously. "But I'm very careful where I wear it."

"Hello, ladies." Flynn slid gracefully around the ottoman so that he was facing the four of us. "What are we talking about?"

"Jewelry," Selene said, tilting her hand down so he could see it. "Have you ever seen such a gorgeous engagement ring?"

"Never." He bent over the ring and whistled. "Fancy. Must have cost a pretty penny."

She lifted her fingers up and gave the ring a proud glance.

"Looks lovely on you," he said.

"Thanks to Beckett." She pointed with her pinkie at the man deep in conversation with Nate on the opposite sofa. "As you know."

"I do know." Flynn grinned. "He's a good guy. One of the best."

"So..." Calista said, fixing Flynn with a look. "You're leaving academia? That's a big decision."

Flynn leaned back and crossed one of his impossibly long legs over the other. He took a swig from his highball glass before answering. "Yep. It's time."

"Did you really mean what you said, that the essays got everything wrong?" She stared at the author.

"No question." He finished the rest of his drink and set the empty glass down on the floor.

"How?" I might as well jump in with both feet.

"Have you read them?"

"Not yet," I admitted, while Calista shook her head. "But I will."

"They're extremely critical. They said I'm doing all of these things that I most certainly am *not* doing, and they missed all of the important things that I *am* doing."

"I understand that it might be strange to read essays about your work," Calista said. "But it's called criticism for a reason."

He laughed. "Very funny. But you and I both know that literary analysis doesn't tend to skewer the author."

"Sometimes it does, though," I said, mentally lining up

examples to share.

"Not like this." Flynn put his palms up in resistance. "These are beyond. Way beyond."

"Don't take this the wrong way, please, but I felt for those poor scholars," Calista said.

"And the editors," I added.

"What do you mean?" He spoke quickly, his eyebrows drawing together in displeasure.

Calista played with a loose thread on her dress. "Just that you devastated them in front of the entire conference."

Flynn pursed his lips. "Well, they were devastating me in front of the entire *world*. None of the reviews were even half as bad as what those scholars wrote. I felt attacked."

"Do you know any of the contributors?" I asked, taking the opportunity to push a little further. "Do you feel that it was personal?"

"No. That's not what I meant. But I'd classify them as willful misreading." He appeared genuinely upset. "You'll see when you read them."

"Did you think the editors are to blame, then?" As long as he would answer, I'd keep asking questions.

"I was thrilled that they even wanted to do the book in the first place. But when I read it..." Flynn shook his head. "It felt as though they had intentionally set me up. Strung me along. Told me how much they thought I'd love the essays. All the while knowing what they were going to publish. And don't forget, they *chose* those. Specifically. So the editors shaped the entire tone."

Calista frowned. "Is it possible that your response has to do with your expectations? Perhaps you expected them to say how great you are, like your fans do every day, and you were surprised when they didn't?"

"It's not that either, though I have to say, that theory sounds a bit condescending."

"I'm sorry. I didn't mean it that way." Calista smiled at him. "Ever since dinner, it's all we can think about. I'm throwing things out to see what sticks to the wall. Just tell us: What *exactly* did they get wrong?"

Our host looked at something behind us and sighed. "You know what? It doesn't matter anymore. I said what I needed to say, and in a few weeks, I'll be done worrying about higher education altogether. I'm out of Fairlake. I need to focus on the series. And luckily, my readers get me. The general population won't be the least bit interested in buying into what some ivory tower analysis is selling. They appreciate me."

Calista nodded, then downed the rest of her drink in one fell swoop.

"Have you spoken to any of your colleagues?" I asked, trying to bring the conversation around to Ellis.

"Well, there's one right there," he said, smiling at Selene.

She smiled back prettily.

He returned his attention to me. "But otherwise, no. Not since dinner."

"I meant before tonight—did they know you were unhappy with the guide?"

"Ellis did."

I tried to keep my facial expression neutral. "How did he know?"

"I emailed him. It was a comprehensive explanation of the issues with a plea for him to take action. But he must not have cared about that because he never wrote me back."

"Did you try again to tell him at the conference?"

"Well, there wasn't much of a chance, was there?" He narrowed his eyes. "Why are you so interested? I'm starting to feel like you're implying something."

"I'm not implying anything. Just trying to figure out what's going on."

"Why?"

"Lila's a sleuth!" Calista said happily, then hiccupped.

"Ah." Flynn gave me an appraising look.

"It's true," Calista insisted. "She has solved *many* crimes."

I stared at her. "I wouldn't say—"

Flynn cut me off. "That may be so, but this is not a game of *Clue*. Ellis was my colleague. Those of us who knew him are genuinely grieving." His face went smooth, like a shutter closing, and his tone went flat. "And for the record, I'm not a murderer."

I nodded. "Sorry. No one is accusing you of anything. Probably time for us to go, Cal," I said firmly, pulling her up and leading her away from the couch.

"I'm sorry," Calista whispered. "I shouldn't have said that. Also, I think I may have had too many drinks."

"Don't worry about it," I said. "Let's just go."

I thanked Flynn for the party as we circled the ottoman.

He didn't respond.

"Speaking of your series, how many more books will you be writing?" Selene rested her elbows on her knees, all glowing anticipation. "Don't think I've mentioned this, but I truly adore your books, Flynn. I've read them all at least five times."

Flynn sat forward abruptly. "No kidding? That's fabulous. Which do you prefer?"

"*The Cave of the Sibyl*. No question. The Prophetess may be my favorite character ever written."

He tucked a wayward strand behind his ear. "She appeared to me in a dream, you know."

"How fascinating." Selene slipped off of the sofa and onto the ottoman next to him. They tipped their heads closely together and were lost to the rest of us almost immediately.

Simone stretched gracefully like a cat. "I think I'll call it a night. We have our little panel tomorrow. Need to be at our best, don't we, to show those judges who should win?" She winked at me.

I took note of her confidence. She wasn't worried about me at all.

As usual.

Chapter 10

Lex was seated at the desk in my room when I returned, flipping through papers. He greeted me absently, but when I sat down on the bed, he moved over quickly.

"How was your night?"

I gave him a detailed description of the whole dinner fiasco and after-party.

He listened closely. "What do you make of all that?"

I took off my earrings and bounced them in my hand while I thought. "There's something strange about that book. First, one of the editors is killed, then the subject of the book he edited rises up unexpectedly and takes everyone who has been involved with it to task in front of the world."

"I concur."

"We need to read the whole thing tonight and figure out what is hidden among its pages."

Waving at the desk, he gave me a regretful smile. "See that pile over there? I have to work on those reports, so you're on your own."

I narrowed my eyes at him. "You manifested some reports to get out of doing your homework?"

"I thought we settled that earlier, remember? Reading is *your* superpower."

"And filling out reports is yours?"

"Evidently. And rather pathetically, come to think of it." He gave me a quick kiss on the cheek and resettled himself at the desk, patting the cover of the book that rested on the corner.

I ignored the gesture and went to brush my teeth first, then changed into sweats and a Stonedale University t-shirt. At least I was going to be comfy during my readathon.

The next morning, I woke with a start when the hotel phone rang. I shot a look at the clock, which read seven a.m. Thank goodness I'd put in a standing order for a wake-up call, as I hadn't set my alarm.

Lex was gone, but he'd left a note on the desk that said he'd text me later.

How romantic.

I took a quick shower and dressed in my professor clothes. Over the years, I'd developed a three-part uniform—a black cotton shirt with black pants or skirt beneath a more formal piece. I could be professional but comfortable in a minute or less without having to spend a lot of thought on the matter other than selecting which jacket or blazer to wear—the choices in my closet ranged from ornately embroidered to monochromatic. Today's was vaguely Victorian: long but nipped in at the waist, with two rows of silver decorative buttons shining against the dark jacquard. After pulling on socks and lace-up ankle boots, I topped the whole thing off with chandelier earrings and called it done.

As I packed my bag for the day, I eyed the critical guide on the nightstand. I'd made it through the introduction and first three sections: biography, essays, and interviews; however, I hadn't had a chance to look at the photographs yet. They weren't what I was most concerned with, anyway, so I was going to count it as having completed my homework.

More or less.

That was the good news.

The bad news was that I hadn't seen anything in there that might shed light on who might have it out for Ellis. And I couldn't figure out exactly what Flynn was up in arms about, either—unless it was a refusal to accept anything less than pure adoration. Maybe he was a perfectionist. Maybe he was overly sensitive. Or maybe he was delusional. In any case, he hadn't handled things well. The introduction written by the editors praised Flynn's work enthusiastically, which made me feel even worse about the way he'd dissed them in public.

My cell phone chirped, and I accepted the call to find Acadia on the other end of the line. She asked me if I would run up to Flynn's room—no one had seen him yet this morning, and he wasn't answering his phone.

"He is supposed to host our Breakfast with the Author event." She paused. "Which I wish we'd never scheduled, in retrospect."

"You didn't know what he would do last night," I said, soothingly, unplugging my charging cord from the socket and rolling it up neatly.

"I still can't believe it. I spent half the night responding to irate emails from numerous attendees."

"I'm sorry."

"Well, it goes with the job." Acadia paused. "Interestingly, there were almost as many emails *praising* our choice of keynote..."

That surprised me.

"...though I suppose it's not that unexpected. There are evaluation challenges for individuals built into the structure of higher education, after all. He seems to have put his finger on the pulse of something. I just wish he hadn't done it in such a public way. Or during *our* conference." She sighed. "Actually, you know what, Lila? I don't even know what I think anymore.

Is this conference going to be famous or infamous? Did Flynn put us on or wipe us off of the academic map? And, by the way, are you as exhausted as I am?"

"Yes, I'm—"

"Whew. Okay. Let's focus. Could you please go check on him right now? Tell him to get downstairs as soon as possible? I'm in the lobby. Sorry to interrupt your plans, but breakfast starts at eight, and I need to go over a few things with him first."

Despite a twinge of trepidation, I accepted my quest as Committee Member On Duty and ran up the stairs and over to Flynn's suite. It didn't matter if he was unhappy to see me. This was my job.

The hallway was quiet, though I could hear showers running and scraps of conversations as I passed different rooms. Just before I reached my destination at the end of the hallway, the dark wood door opened and Selene Raleigh tiptoed out.

In the same stained olive-green suit as she'd been wearing the night before.

With a raging case of bedhead.

She caught sight of me and froze. Then she tried to unobtrusively press down her hair in the back under the guise of fiddling with her nametag cord. We both knew she'd been caught in the act of sneaking out, but she nodded as if she were a queen greeting a visiting diplomat. "Good morning, Lila."

"Good morning, Selene." I smiled and stepped aside.

"I was just chatting with Flynn about his keynote speech," she informed me, as she began to pass.

"Ah. How kind."

"Yes. Always happy to help out a colleague." She lifted her chin and started to sweep away, but stopped and turned back, with narrowed eyes. "Wait. What are *you* doing here?"

"Official conference business," I said.

She waited.

"Sworn to secrecy, I'm afraid."

"Fine." She exhaled heavily and flounced away. "See you at the panel," she threw over her shoulder, haughtily.

I put my hand against the door just before it closed all the way and knocked briskly.

"Come in."

When I stepped inside the dark room, Flynn was stirring a cup of coffee. "Hello, lover. Back for more? I'm game." He set the spoon down on the counter and looked up as he took a sip of the steaming liquid. Like Selene, he froze, then tried to act like nothing had happened.

He tightened the towel around his waist while I attempted to look anywhere but at his washboard abs. "Morning, Lila. What can I do for you?"

"Acadia sent me to collect you for the breakfast event."

"Right. I'm on my way. Just need to throw on some clothes—it'll only take a minute. Make yourself comfortable." He disappeared down one of the hallways.

I hadn't planned to escort him, but I might as well make sure he found his way to Acadia. Perching on one of the armless dining chairs, I stared out the window at the mountains. Then I popped up again and went over to the fireplace. Might as well have a look, though I knew I didn't have much time. Glasses were sitting on every conceivable surface, and the room reeked of alcohol. I longed to scoop everything up, just to restore some order, but it wasn't my space to maintain.

I scanned all the surfaces and didn't find anything of interest.

Until I came upon a note, written in red ink, sticking out from under a laptop. The handwriting swooped and soared across the page. I read it quickly:

We need to talk. Call me as soon as you wake up. It's

urgent.

"Ready?" Flynn strolled into the room, clad in another one of his flowy-shirt-and-rock-star-pant combos. I crumpled the note in my hand and tried to look innocent.

"After you," I said, slipping the note into my pocket when he turned around.

We moved down the hallway quietly. As we waited for the elevator, he cleared his throat. "Hey, sorry if I was rude last night. The whole evening was very emotional for me. I was all over the place."

"I understand. Thanks. I hope today is more relaxing."

He smiled as a soft ping announced the elevator's arrival. Once we were inside and the doors closed, I was wrapped in a cloud of mint.

"Is that mint scent from the hotel soap?" If so, they were stocking the VIP suite with a whole different product. The tiny bottles in my room had smelled like an odd blend of oranges and bubble gum.

"I don't use soap," he said.

Ewww. Why would he tell me that?

"It's a special liquid cleanser that my natural grocer sells."

"Ah."

"Fancy a product demonstration?" He delivered this with a wolfish grin while scanning me up and down. "I'd *love* to lather you up."

Double ewww.

I returned what I hoped was a withering look. "Flynn, mere moments ago, I bumped into someone walking out of your hotel room. How can you even *think* that—"

"Sorry." He winced. "Sometimes I can't turn it off."

"What do you mean?"

He shifted his weight and studied the floor. "I'm a total

introvert. When I have to do the public author thing, the only way I can handle it is by sort of becoming this other...person."

"Well, that other person doesn't have to be a *creeper*."

"I know. It's like I'm not even aware I'm doing it."

"Are you talking about another personality?"

"More like a persona."

I stared at him.

"Look, the books got popular so fast that everything went a little out of control. The public relations people and press constructed me as a player. Then they encouraged me to embrace it. For social media purposes. They think it sells books. You know, action hero gets the girl—" He lifted the heavy silver pendant hanging from a cord around his neck and let it fall backwards so that it hit his chest with a thud, as if he were punishing himself. "Ugh. It doesn't even make sense. I'm not the action hero. I'm just the writer."

He swung the pendant again. "Sometimes I don't even know who I am anymore. I'm truly sorry."

"I appreciate the context."

"And, by the way, it's not what you think with Selene. I'm not that kind of guy, no matter what you've heard about me."

Or what he'd orchestrated himself as part of his author act? "But the—"

The elevator doors pinged and opened. Acadia was waiting to bustle him off to the breakfast. She thanked me and led Flynn away before he could say anything else.

Shortly afterwards, I was seated with Nate and Calista at a corner table. I had marched into The Path's End restaurant intending to order oatmeal, but somehow my order translated itself to go with the flow after my friends had ordered waffles.

How does that happen, anyway? If someone could figure

out how to keep one's willpower on a leash, they'd be a gazillionaire.

"Sleep well, all?" I poured butter pecan syrup over the golden squares in front of me. They smelled heavenly.

They both nodded, mouths full, chewing happily.

"These are the best waffles I've ever had," Calista said. "The rumors were true."

"There were rumors?" I said through a mouthful of deliciousness.

"Yes. And you know what other rumors are afoot?" Nate asked, his eyes twinkling. "That you're up for an award."

"Why didn't you tell us?" Calista asked as she cut another piece of waffle. "I mean, I heard about it and texted Aunt Vi. You didn't tell her either."

"I didn't tell anyone." I swallowed and took a sip of water. "I don't even really know what it is."

"It's the New Voices Prize," Calista said. "And you're going to win."

"No, I'm not. No way. But they announced it at the welcome banquet, out of the blue. I didn't even know it was a thing before that."

"And you'll be on the special panel today, right?"

"Yes, and I'm already wishing I could skip it."

Calista put down her fork. "Why?"

"I don't know, exactly. It's not about the award, which I only learned about yesterday, so that part seems altogether unreal. It's about..." I took a deep breath and let it out slowly, trying to calm my nerves and zoom in on the cause for them simultaneously. "Probably because the panelists are Simone, Selene, Beckett, and me. One of these things is not like the other, you know?"

"You're every bit as good as they are," Calista said indignantly. "Better, in my opinion."

"You're sweet. And biased. But they're already a unit, with similar backgrounds. And don't get me wrong, Calista. We had fun growing up, never landing in one place for too long. It was an adventure." I smiled at my cousin, who had lived with us after her parents passed away. We'd moved around the country as my mother careened from one art gig to another.

"We did. I wouldn't trade it for anything." She turned to Nate. "Of course, we didn't have any money. Not a dime. Aunt Vi does now, though. She's rich."

I hadn't thought about it that way before, but Calista was right. "She doesn't flaunt it."

"That makes all the difference," she agreed. "And she gives a lot away, even though she works very hard to earn it."

"Look, I'm not saying that people shouldn't have money," I protested. "It's not that at all. It's about..."

"Go on," Nate urged.

"Behavior. Sometimes the way the Raleighs act gets to me."

"Um. It gets to *everyone*," Nate said. "Most of us didn't grow up in actual mansions with buckets of gold lying around everywhere."

"Buckets of gold?" Calista laughed.

"You know what I mean. Über-ostentatiousness Land." He waved his knife and returned to cutting his next bite.

"Mmm hmm." I hesitated. "But I was thinking more of how they are so very sure of themselves at all times. Super confident."

"You might even say entitled," Calista said, adding another splash of syrup to her plate.

"Yes, that's the right word," Nate agreed. "So how does that translate into you wanting to skip your panel?"

"Somehow their excessive confidence—"

"Massive sense of entitlement," my cousin interjected.

"—flusters me at times. That's all. And this is public. I don't want to look like an idiot up there," I said, slicing into a blueberry.

They both reassured me that I wouldn't look like an idiot.

"Even if you do, we will love you," Nate pronounced, then caught himself. "Wait. I'm not saying that you *will* look like an idiot. I'm saying that no matter what happens, we will still love you." He winced. "No, that's not right either. Obviously, I need more coffee." He threw his hands into the air. "Please ignore what I just said and listen to this instead: everything you do is right and everything they do is wrong."

I laughed. "That's definitely *not* true. Though something strange did happen this morning." I waved it away. "Never mind. I'll just do my best. It's all I can do. That's my lifelong mantra, anyway."

"Exactly right. Now what are you not telling us?" Calista paused, fork halfway to her mouth.

"I don't know if I should—"

Nate tapped the knife against his water glass. "Lila, it's us. Your most trusted confidants. You not only *should* but you *must*."

"You have to keep it to yourselves," I warned them.

They promised and leaned forward expectantly as I described Selene's departure from Flynn's room. Calista's mouth fell open and Nate's eyes widened.

"Oh man, poor Beckett." He shook his head. "I know you just made us swear on our firstborns—"

"I did not!"

"—but I feel like I should tell him, Lila."

I'd momentarily forgotten that Nate and Selene's fiancé were longtime friends. Oops.

"Nate, please don't say anything."

"I'll have to think about it."

"Are you sure they were together?" Calista stared at me. "I

mean: *together* together?"

"Well, when I walked into the room, he thought I was her and asked if I was back for more. The implication was clear. But Flynn said to me later that it wasn't what I thought. Or that he wasn't what I thought. It was a little confusing. In fact, the whole conversation was strange."

"How so—"

"We're going to have to put a pin in that, Nate," Calista said, tapping her watch, "because it's almost time for the panel. Go get 'em, Lil."

"It is? I need to do something first," I said. "Meet you there."

Chapter 11

The panel was set up like every other one at the conference: two long tables on a riser at the front of the room. A cardboard nameplate identified each scholar's place, and there were glasses and a pitcher of water waiting for us to share. Rows of folding chairs filled the rest of the room. Although I'd arrived a few minutes early, not a single empty seat remained, and there were individuals standing along the back wall.

My stomach flipped and I turned to go back out into the hallway, only to come face to face with the Raleighs. Simone paused to speak with me, but Selene swept by. Beckett gave me a rueful smile—a silent acknowledgment of his fiancée's icy blast—and followed in her wake as if towed by a rope.

"Are we ready, Lila?" Simone's crossed arms hugged a black three-ring binder to her chest. A matching binder had been delivered to my hotel room while I was at the after-party, with instructions to bring my current manuscript to the panel today.

They were *really* making up this thing as they went along.

Not great for the nerves, honestly.

I'd been too tired last night to do anything about it, so I'd had to pop into the "business office" of the hotel—which had two ancient desktop computers, two newer printers, a pair of scissors, a stapler and a three-hole punch—after breakfast. I'd punched holes into my pages as fast as I could and shoved them into the binder. I'd managed to swing it, but these requirements were definitely ratcheting up the pressure.

Simone's eyes roved over the audience. "I love reading in public. There's just something about the crowd hanging on your every word."

Hanging on your every word? That had not been my experience. Mostly, I tried to will them to remain in their seats at least until I'd finished.

"You did a fine job the other day," she said. "At your panel."

I waited for the forthcoming burn, the drop of acid that sizzled as it landed.

She smiled at me.

"Thank you," I murmured, but I was confused. I knew how to handle the agenda-propelled insult-wrapped-inside-a-compliment Simone. This new version was throwing me for a loop.

Then again, maybe that was her plan all along.

She gave a shimmy of excitement. "Ooh. They're waving at us. It's almost showtime."

Simone strutted up to the table, nimbly ascended the riser, and took a seat next to Beckett, who was farthest away from us. As I followed, I tripped over a cord on the floor and headed for a face plant. With a crouching quick step, I somehow managed to stop myself halfway and wrench my body upwards.

Which was all well and good, except that I appeared to be bowing to my panel mates.

In front of everyone.

Perfect.

I climbed the steps and fell into my seat next to Selene, who was repositioning the microphone between us, and tried to regain some dignity by acting like nothing had happened. When I leaned forward to retrieve the binder from my bag, I hit my forehead on the mic, which squealed loudly. The audience members covered their ears as I apologized.

Selene snickered at the success of her little prank. I didn't bother to look at her as I put my fingers to the spot on my head that was surely turning red at that very moment. It was tender but not bleeding, so I had no excuse to run from the room. Sadly. At least it had distracted me from the butterflies that had previously been using my stomach as a punching bag. So there was that.

I couldn't figure out what Selene was up to, though. Wouldn't you think that if you'd been caught cheating on your fiancé, you'd not try to infuriate the one person who could tell the world? She seemed to be doing the opposite, orchestrating a microphone injury. That was not a normal thing to do. Was she daring me to say something? Did she *want* the world to know? Or maybe she wanted to break up with Beckett but didn't have the guts, so was tricking me into doing her dirty work for her?

I shook my head to clear that line of reasoning and sucked in my breath at the sharp pain emanating from what was surely, by now, a highly noticeable mark that was gaining visibility by the second. No worries. I'd just do my reading with a giant red circle on my forehead. It was the inside part I was worrying about now.

Note to self: no sudden movements.

Second note to self: start carrying a hat in case of head injury.

A wave of dizziness passed over me. My brain seemed to be on overload. It was either the nervousness about the panel or Selene had knocked me into delirious mode.

I gripped the table to center myself and counted to ten. She was *not* going to beat me before I even got started.

A flutter in my peripheral vision drew my attention. Calista and Nate gave me thumbs-ups from their chairs in the middle of the room. They made faces too—my cousin blew me a kiss and Nate did what I thought at first was some sort of strong-man imitation, his version of telling me to be strong.

Then I realized he was mouthing "Hulk smash." I giggled. That helped.

Even if it triggered another blast of pain in my injury site.

Lex slipped into the room and leaned against the back wall. He winked at me. That helped too.

Acadia moved swiftly down the center aisle and joined us onstage, positioning herself at the midpoint of the table. "Welcome, everyone. Thank you for joining us for the first-ever New Voices Award panel. Our judges, who will not be revealed until after the award has been determined, are here with us now. The structure for this panel is as follows. Each author will read for ten minutes. When all four authors have presented, they will take questions from the audience on their topics. You should have found some index cards on your chairs when you came in. As you listen to the panelists read, please feel free to write down your questions. They'll be collected after the readings. Then I'll ask some of your questions, blended in with"—she held up a bundle of index cards—"questions from the judges, which I have already gathered. And now, I'd like to introduce our panelists. All of them have books forthcoming from Fairlake University Press."

She gestured to the far end of the table. "First, we have Dr. Beckett Standhouse."

"The third," Selene said loudly, just as she had when introducing him at the book signing. She was really invested in that, I guess.

Acadia blinked a few times and continued. "Beckett is an assistant professor at Fairlake University and author of *War Imagery in the Work of Flynn McMaster*." She went on to list the academic journals in which he had published articles. The majority of them, I noticed, were on Flynn McMaster.

Beckett blushed furiously and bobbed his head throughout her entire introduction, as if he were listening to a song through an invisible pair of earplugs.

"Next, we have Dr. Simone Raleigh and Dr. Selene Raleigh, co-authors of *Brontë and Dare: Double Trouble*. Selene is also at Fairlake University, and Simone is from Stonedale University. Both are assistant professors." She gave the title of a chapter scheduled to appear in another anthology, also co-written by the sisters.

The twins gave those odd sideways waves like they were princesses passing by the commoners in a carriage. Dainty and indifferent.

"Finally, Dr. Lila Maclean, assistant professor at Stonedale University, is the author of *Beyond the Veil: Isabella Dare and the Gothic*." I dipped my head once, slowly, and tried to smile. That was all I could manage. My face was aflame and my head had begun to throb.

Acadia paused. "I hadn't realized until I read those introductions aloud how perfectly balanced this is: we have two professors from Stonedale University and two from Fairlake University. May the best school win!"

I hadn't even considered the representing-our-school part until now. Added pressure, that. I was sure Chancellor Wellington would have an opinion on the subject.

The audience turned their full attention to us. I'd never felt more like a pet waiting to be adopted.

"Let's mix things up, shall we?" Acadia asked, sounding like she was proposing something daring. "Rather than just going down the line, we'll work from the outside in. Lila, why don't you go first, then Beckett, then Simone and Selene, in whichever order you two prefer."

I opened my binder slowly and began to read. While I may

have looked calm on the outside, my heart was racing along with my thoughts on the inside. I concentrated on keeping my voice steady—it has a tendency to quaver when I read my own writing aloud in front of a crowd—and remembering to breathe.

Using a trick someone had taught me about keeping my eyes on the page until the initial wave of nerves passed, I read the first two pages focusing intently on the words. I dared to look up at that point and realized that the audience was smiling and nodding enthusiastically. My muscles began to relax and the reading became easier and more enjoyable. The rest of the selection went by in a blur, and after I said the last word, there was a burst of loud applause.

Beckett went next—and although he cleared his throat for almost a full minute upfront and his face turned beet-red, he soon settled into a smooth pattern, his pleasant voice and sense of humor winning over the crowd. We all applauded eagerly for him.

When he was done, Simone smiled at the crowd before beginning, which was an advantage. There was no doubt that the twins were drop-dead gorgeous. All that Beckett and I could do was hope the judges weren't factoring our looks into the equation. He was handsome enough, but they were Grace Kelly clones, with allure in spades. Simone read a lively section about *Jane Eyre,* and the audience seemed to hang on her every word, just like she'd predicted they would. If she ever wanted a job as some sort of on-air talent, I was sure she could land one in a snap. In general, I'd wager, she could pretty much do anything she wanted. At the conclusion, she bowed her head gracefully.

Selene applauded along with everyone else and turned to face the audience.

"I—" She stopped, her mouth half-open, then her hand flew to her neck and she pitched forward onto her binder, her head twisted toward her sister. The room gasped.

Simone put her arm on her twin's back and called out her name. She peered into her face and screamed for help.

The room exploded with activity all at once. Acadia whipped her phone out and was talking to someone immediately. Some people turned to their neighbors and asked what was going on. Others jumped to their feet and ran out. Still more stayed, milling around anxiously. Throughout, Simone was gently shaking her sister.

"She's breathing," she said. "Thank God."

"Should we sit her up?" I asked, worried about her position.

"I don't think she should be moved," Acadia said. "You're supposed to leave people where they are when they're in an accident."

Beckett ignored that and pulled Selene backwards out of the chair into his arms. He sank down onto the floor behind the table where we'd been sitting and cradled her, crooning something quietly. We formed a circle around her, watching closely. She looked oddly serene but uncannily still. Like a beautiful, terrifying doll.

I heard Lex's voice telling people to go out into the hallway. Gradually, the room quieted, and he came around the riser to join us.

He surveyed the situation, introduced himself as Detective Archer, and asked what happened.

"She fainted or something," Beckett said. "Out of nowhere."

"Has she fainted before?" Lex asked Simone, who was kneeling next to her sister, holding her hand.

She didn't take her eyes off of Selene's face.

Lex tried again. "I'm sorry, Simone, but we need to ask. Is there anything we should know about? Does she have a history of fainting?"

Simone shook her head. "She's quite healthy, physically. Never gets sick."

Just then, Selene stirred. She blinked slowly, opened her eyes, and shrank back when she saw all of us gazing down at her. "What's happening?" She sounded scared.

"You passed out, honey." Beckett spoke to her gently. "Can you sit?" He tilted her slightly and she stayed there, looking confusedly up at us.

"Here," Acadia said, thrusting a small bottle of orange juice at Selene. "This should help."

"Thank you," Selene moved into a sitting position, unscrewed the cap and, after a few sips, gave a decisive nod. "I'm feeling better now. So sorry, everyone."

We all reassured her that it was fine.

"Oh! We were in the middle of the panel." Tears welled up in her eyes. "I ruined it, didn't I?"

"No," Simone sat down next to her. "You're fine. Don't worry about it."

"But how can someone win now?" She wiped her cheeks.

"No one cares about winning," I said. "We're just glad you're okay."

Selene gave me a suspicious look, as if she didn't quite believe me.

"I mean it."

"Thank you, Lila."

The paramedics burst into the room, evaluated Selene, and dismissed us. Lex and I moved toward the back row, where Richmond and Candace were waiting with solemn faces.

As I walked past the empty chairs, a text came in from Calista, saying that I'd done a great job and asking me to please send her an update as soon as I could. She and Nate were worried about me. There were a lot of heart emojis at the end of her message.

"Everything okay up there, Detective Archer?" Richmond's hearty voice belied his appearance. His suit was wrinkled and his pocket square hung from its perch as if dejected.

"Appears to be," Lex affirmed. "She's regained consciousness."

"Good news." He pulled a small cloth out of an inside pocket and unfolded it. "Good, good, good."

"We've been sitting back here feeling quite helpless," Candace said. Her hands were clasped together in her lap, giving her a composed air, but she'd missed a button and her whole jacket was off-kilter, with a gap at her sternum. "And hoping that it wasn't anything like...you know...the other night."

"Candace means she hopes it wasn't fatal. No chance of that, right?" Richmond gaped at Lex.

"Not as far as we know. It doesn't appear to be serious."

"Excellent," Richmond said, wiping his glasses with the cloth. "Speaking of the other night, any theories on what happened to Ellis?"

"We're following up on leads," Lex said. "As you may have heard, Ellis was hit with a metal bar. It looks to have been wiped clean but we're still analyzing it. We've conducted interviews with a number of people."

"In other words, you have no idea," Richmond drawled. He held his glasses up to the light and squinted through them.

"I'd say we're in the middle of the process," Lex said tightly.

"Again, I'm so sorry for your loss," I said to the editors.

Candace's eyes shone with tears. "Thank you, Lila."

Oh no. I hadn't meant to make her cry again. I tried to move to safer topics.

"You both have said that you knew him for years, right? Can you think of anyone who would have wanted to attack him?"

"No," Richmond said. "He didn't really get into tangles with other people. Bit of a loner. He just liked to sit in his office and read literature and write about it."

"Very good scholar," Candace added. "Renowned in his

field, actually."

"How was he as a teacher?" Lex inquired.

They stared at each other, silently conferring.

Richmond gave in first. "Not the strongest, if I'm being honest. Students often complained that all he does is lecture."

"Which used to be considered a perfectly legitimate teaching method," Candace said. "For decades. But nowadays, there's pressure to be more interactive. You know what I mean, Lila."

I nodded.

"He was talking about retiring next year, anyway. Wanted to go down to Florida and get a little house on the beach with his wife."

A wave of sadness went through me.

"Long overdue, if you ask me. We're both turning seventy this year." Richmond's face changed, perhaps as he realized that Ellis would not be celebrating his next birthday.

Lex went on. "Aside from working on the book, did you spend time together?"

Richmond emitted something between a cough and a bark. "Absolutely. We were colleagues both on and off campus."

"Our families vacationed together last year." Candace pressed her fingertips just below her eyes. "He was a great husband, father, and friend."

"We did." Richmond nodded in agreement. "We talked about our book on the beach, remember?"

"He was so excited." She looked at Richmond. "I don't know what we'll do without him, going forward."

Richmond sniffed and his shoulders slumped. "Don't even know if there is a way forward. Not after what Flynn did last night."

"True." Candace patted his shoulder. "But let's try not to think about that right now."

"Can't you just ignore what Flynn said?" I asked. "It's only his opinion, anyway. Who says he gets to decide?"

Richmond stared at me. "It's his opinion, true, but since he's the toast of the town at present, and visible on a grand scale, it goes a long way. A very long way."

"Even longer on social media." Candace shook her head. "Hanover is doing his best—he hasn't budged from his hotel room since the dinner, if you can believe it, because he's been working so hard—but there's only so much that he can do. Flynn's speech went viral."

"What about no publicity is bad publicity? That's a thing, right?" I heard myself reversing what I'd said after the dinner, but suddenly I saw the value of the sentiment—it's useful for when there's nothing else to say and you have to dredge it up in order to be able to say anything at all.

"It is," Candace agreed.

"Or isn't there one about waiting for the *next* news cycle because everyone will then forget about *this* news cycle?" I was having trouble coming up with the exact words, but there had to be something that would make them feel better.

"It's heartbreaking," Richmond said. "You have no idea how hard we had to fight to make this series happen. First the university, then the board of trustees—and oh, the hoops that had to be jumped through for funding. Many people couldn't see the vision."

Candace took up the thread. "We thought we were so blessed to have access to a superstar like Flynn. Thought the critical guides would sell themselves. How ironic."

"Didn't they sell out this weekend?" I asked softly.

"That's true." She closed her eyes for a moment.

Richmond harrumphed. "In a nutshell, it was a coup. We knew it, he knew it, and so did everyone else. It was a tremendous launch. Then for him to just decimate it—us—in that way. With one speech. It was a knockout."

"We never saw it coming." Candace looked down, noticed the gap in her jacket, and repositioned her hands over it coolly. She was genuinely unflappable.

"In any case, we're done with the series now. He saw to that." Richmond studied his fingernails. "I'd also like to do a recall of all the books we sold this weekend. Erase the whole thing. Forget it ever happened."

Candace swung her head around. "You can't, Richmond."

He met her eyes and shook his head sadly. "I know. It's not up to me, anyway. We need to give that money to the investors. And it wouldn't be fair to the scholars who are published there, either. At least they'll get some good out of it. As long as their schools don't hear the negative review that Flynn gave their chapters, that is."

We all pondered the damage that Flynn had done. The ripples moving outward would have an impact on a number of other people's lives.

When everything went quiet, it seemed like a good time to gather up my things from the table. Excusing myself, I hurried over to the riser and slid the binder into my satchel. As I fastened the flap, I saw Selene's binder resting on the table. Perhaps Richmond and Candace would want to hold onto it.

I picked it up, went down the stairs, and promptly tripped on the same cord from before. This time, I did a full face plant.

In front of my boyfriend *and* publisher.

Not optimal.

Seeing them lurch forward in their chairs, arms reached out as if they could catch me, I assured them that I was unhurt and begged them to stay in their seats.

Gingerly, I did a reverse inchworm and righted myself, reaching over to get Selene's binder, which had fallen open.

I did a double take.

Settling the binder in my lap, I flipped back to the beginning and went through, page by page.

They were all blank.

Chapter 12

As soon as we walked out of the room, I asked Lex if we could go to Scarlett's Café, one of my favorite places in Stonedale. I desperately needed a break from this conference. He happened to have a lull in his schedule and whisked me off-site immediately. One jangle of the door chimes and two steps into the warmth of the fragrant, cozy restaurant, and I knew we'd made the right decision.

The large sugar-free caramel latte delivered much-needed caffeine to my very core.

The muffin that followed further enhanced my emotional state.

The ibuprofen that tamped down the pounding headache made it a trifecta.

I sighed happily.

"Better?" Lex studied me from across the booth, one arm slung along the top of the red vinyl bench, the other holding a mug of steaming coffee.

"You have no idea."

He set the mug down and reached his hand out for mine. "How are your knees? That was a pretty hard fall."

"They're fine."

"And how's your—" He gestured toward my forehead.

"Head wound?" The mirror in his car had confirmed a red circle, but it wasn't as bright as I'd imagined.

"Also fine, and thank you for your concern."

"Always."

"You know I'm tough, though."

"If you say so." He squeezed my fingers once before letting go and picking up his coffee again.

"What do you mean, Lex? I'm *tough.*"

"You are. Just not..." A smile played over his lips. "Cop tough."

"Fair enough. But definitely...professor tough."

"Absolutely."

"And now that I'm fortified by caffeine and my synapses are crackling again, let's talk about our interview."

His eyebrows went up.

"You know, the interview? With Candace and Richmond?"

"Ah. Yes."

"Isn't that what you call it?"

"Sure. Go ahead. What did you think?"

"They seemed fond of Ellis. They didn't know who else might have had it in for him."

"Agreed." Lex toyed with the spoon in front of him, thinking. "There doesn't seem to be any conflicts among the three editors. And we've looked all over social media too—"

"I was going to suggest that. If we weren't at this conference where every second of every day was accounted for, I'd have done it already."

He smiled. "We've completed a sweep. There's nothing to indicate any discord there. No trolling, no complaining, no arguments—on his pages or those of his colleagues. We've spoken to people at the university and to his family as well."

Through the window, I watched a blackbird hopping across the sidewalk outside. There didn't seem to be any rhyme or reason to where it went.

Kind of like this investigation.

"Could this have been a random act of violence? Someone who happened to be walking through that room the same time as Ellis and took a swing at him?"

Lex rubbed his eyes. "It's possible. Could have been a spur-of-the-moment assault. You never know what will set someone off."

"Where did the metal bar come from?"

"Chair leg. The hotel manager said one of the staff was mid-repair and was called away to help out with a spill in another location. By the time he returned, the leg had been used as a weapon."

"Wow. Was anyone else seen in the room beforehand?"

"No one was scheduled to be in there at that time. Doesn't mean they weren't. Just means they weren't required to be."

I drank the last of my latte. "So no one was observed going into or out of the room."

He shook his head. "But no one was watching, either."

I shot up in my seat. "What about cameras in the hotel? Don't they have those for security?"

"In the lobby, near doors, and at check in. They don't cover the whole floor."

I slumped down. Then I perked up again. "We still have the book."

Lex scratched his forehead. "What are you proposing?"

"Perhaps there's an aspect of his editorial work that made someone angry."

"Maybe someone didn't like his tone in an email, you're saying?" He appeared dubious.

"Could be. Or they didn't like how their chapter was edited."

"Would that make someone murderous?"

"You'd be surprised at how strongly people feel about editing suggestions," I said gravely.

"So there's that..."

"Or," I snapped my fingers at a dawning realization, "maybe it's not about who is in the book at all."

He looked confused.

"Maybe it's who's *not* in it."

I pulled out my phone and wrote an email to Richmond and Candace, asking if they would be willing to provide a list of the people who had submitted to the Flynn McMaster project.

When I looked up, Lex waved his coffee mug. "Fill me in?"

"When someone wants to put together a collection of critical essays, they usually send out a call for papers. Scholars submit whatever is required—usually an abstract or short summary of the argument, sometimes the chapter itself. Then the essays that work best together are selected by the editor or, in this case, editors."

"And..."

"They only chose five essays for the guide, and we know there were *many* more than that. This was, by all accounts, a prestigious and visible project and, well, you've seen firsthand how people love Flynn. There must have been numerous scholars dying to get in."

He gave me a pointed look.

"No pun intended," I said. "Oh, that's horrible. Sorry."

"Go on. How does this help us?"

"All the people who were rejected may be harboring some resentment. So if we can find any names on the list of submitters who are also attendees of this conference, we could have a proper suspect."

"Got it." He nodded approvingly. "Well done, Professor. Anything else you can think of?"

"Two things, actually."

Lex leaned back. "I'm listening."

"First, I wanted to show you this." I scrambled around in

my satchel and withdrew Selene's binder, which Richmond and Candace had asked me to return to her. I placed it in front of Lex. "At the panel, we were each supposed to read an excerpt from our books. The Raleighs are co-writing theirs, which is divided into two sections, so they each brought a binder with their half. Simone read from hers, and Selene was supposed to go next. But..." I pointed to the notebook. "Open it."

He flipped the cover with an air of amusement. I had the feeling he was humoring me. But as he began to leaf through the blank pages, his expression turned serious.

"You can stop now. They're all the same."

"So," he raised his head slowly, "she didn't bring anything to read."

"Correct."

"Why?"

"I don't know, Lex. It may be a simple mistake. Perhaps she grabbed the wrong notebook. Or"—I sat up straighter, stuck by a thought—"perhaps she brought this blank binder on purpose."

"Why would she do that?"

"Because she didn't *have* anything to bring."

I expected him to gasp at my insight but it soon became clear that he didn't understand the importance.

"What I'm saying is, she didn't *write* anything for the project. At all. Ever."

"Strange." Lex pushed the binder back toward me.

"Please be more excited. This is a big deal."

"Why?"

"Because it shows that she was trying to fake a presentation. She is up for an award for the book that she was supposed to read from. For which she has a publishing contract. And yet, there is no evidence that her part of the book exists. Doesn't that seem odd to you?"

"Selene could have just not printed out her chapters, Lila.

Maybe she didn't have time, so she used a ream of paper from the business center to make it appear as though she was fulfilling the competition guidelines."

He was right. The blank book didn't prove anything, really, no matter how peculiar it was. "But she was supposed to read from it."

"Maybe she just wanted to wing it. Some people thrive on spontaneity. Or rule-breaking."

"Okay, Detective. You've made your point."

He smiled at me. "We're on the same team, Lila."

What an annoying saying. It was right up there with "calm down," or "your imagination is running wild," or "stop acting like coffee is the answer to everything." But we had a criminal to catch, so I'd give him a pass this time.

"Oh, wait!" I pulled out the note I'd found in Flynn's room. "Does this seem like anything?"

He studied the writing on the paper. "How did you get this?"

I told him about Acadia sending me on the mission to retrieve Flynn from his hotel room.

"But why did you take it?"

"It could be a clue."

Lex shook his head. "We don't take things from people's rooms, Lila. That's not how it's done."

Oops.

"There's a protocol." An edge crept into his tone.

"I'm sorry about that. I thought it might be helpful if we knew who was upset with him. Maybe they pushed him to speak out."

"Yes, that would be helpful, but we have to follow the rules." He looked down at the square of paper again. "Having said that, any idea who wrote this? Do you think it was Selene? Didn't you say she was in there alone with Flynn this morning?"

"Yes." I'd caught him up to speed on the car ride over.

"Any idea what her handwriting looks like?"

"No, I've only seen Simone's. And it's not even close."

"What do you mean?"

I turned my hand palm up so he could place the paper on it, which he did. Then I pointed to the large loops of the ink. "These are distinctive. The swirls are...carefree."

"Carefree?"

"That's not the right term, but you know what I mean. They're loose. Flowing."

"Okay, and..." He rolled his hand, urging me to continue.

"Simone's writing is very tight and controlled. Cramped, even. I don't know how she reads it, frankly." I'd tried to puzzle out notes she'd left on a document once—when we were forced to work together, as co-advisors of Literature Club—and had ended up having to talk to her about it instead.

"Do you think Selene's handwriting would be similar?"

"Because they're twins? No. That doesn't mean their handwriting has to be the same." I folded my napkin into a tiny square as I thought. "Which means that the note-writer could be Selene. Or anyone else in the world, I guess. We need to keep our eyes peeled for—"

"Carefree swirlers?" His lips quirked. "On the many notes for comparison we'll be finding around the ranch in the future?"

"Never mind. You're right." My clue had turned out to be a dud.

"But speaking of Selene, what's your take on her fainting spell?"

"It seemed real while it was happening. But everything changed after I found the binder. Now I don't know."

He sat back and stared into the distance, just over my shoulder. I could almost see the cogs moving as he processed this new information. Finally, he flicked his eyes back to me.

"All right. Filing that information away for future examination. And you said there were two things. Even though it feels like we just did two things—"

"There was a detour," I admitted.

"—so what's the next one?""

"We haven't discussed the fact that we know there is someone who has a big problem with the Fairlake book and told us so: Flynn McMaster. Everyone heard that."

"That's true. We did ask him some questions as a colleague of Ellis, but that was before the keynote. If the book is truly at the center of all this, then perhaps we need to have another talk with Mr. Action Movie."

I arched an eyebrow. "Do I detect a note of...something?"

"Jealousy? Nah. But he's a character, isn't he?"

"Not a fan of the pirate vibe?"

Lex gave me a long look. "Are you?"

"Hmmm." I tilted my head, pretending to think. "Not really. I'm more into detective couture."

He smiled and patted the sleeve of his jacket. "Last year's collection."

"And worth every penny," I said, smiling.

As we drove up the winding road through the arched wrought-iron Tattered Star Ranch gates, my phone pinged with a reminder.

I turned to Lex. "We've got the tour in an hour. You know, the one where they walk us through the property and show us all the places where famous scenes were shot?"

We'd bought tickets a month ago, as the tours often sold out.

"I'm not going to be able to make it, Lila. You brought up a good point about Flynn. I need to ask him some more questions."

"Oh, forget the tour, then. I'd rather come with you."

"Actually," he gave me an apologetic look, "I'll be taking this one myself. From what you told me about your discussion with Flynn during the elevator ride, I don't think your presence will work with the tone I'm going to use."

"But he was kind of opening up to me—"

"Exactly. I'm going to come in more formally than I could if you were with me. Sometimes it helps when a suspect thinks something is happening behind the scenes, officially speaking. If they get nervous, sometimes they talk more."

"Or less."

"It could go either way. But I have a gut feeling about this."

"Sure." I stared out the window at the pine trees until he parked.

"Please don't take it personally. And you need to rendezvous with the Fairlake people anyway, right? Find out about that list?"

"Yes. Okay, I'm on the case."

That was the end of the conversation until we were inside, on the elevator.

"Good luck to you, Professor," he said, leaning over and giving me a quick kiss.

"And to you, Detective." I gave him an even longer kiss back.

We spent the rest of the ride up to the tenth floor thus occupied.

The doors slid open and Lex stepped out. Flynn would be facing a challenge if he had anything to hide. The detective had his game face on.

I rode the elevator back down to the lobby. Since I didn't know Selene's room number, I was going to leave the notebook at the main desk for her.

As I crossed the lobby, I caught sight of the twins walking through the front door, rendering my phone call unnecessary. When they drew closer, however, I saw that they appeared to be arguing.

I ducked behind a large potted plant as they passed.

"I don't know what you want me to do," Selene—according to her nametag—said.

"Well, you can't put this one on me," Simone replied.

"I can't believe you're saying all this. It's very stressful, you know."

"But what did you think would happen?"

When they were slightly farther away, their conversation appeared to intensify. They faced each other, both gesticulating angrily, then abruptly went in different directions. Selene took a sharp left down a hallway, and Simone headed back toward me. I emerged unobtrusively—I hoped—from my hiding spot and posed with my cell phone to create a posture of nonchalance.

When she saw me, her whole demeanor transformed. She might have been full of rage, but she was the picture of tranquility. I'd figured out this much in our years together: Simone Raleigh never wanted to appear out of control. She needed to be in charge of everything at all times, including herself.

And it was frightening how quickly she appeared to switch emotional states.

"Lila," she said calmly. "Thank you for helping with my sister today."

"How is she doing? What happened?"

"She fainted. The paramedics said she was a tad dehydrated. She's fine now, though. Hydrated and resting."

Well, that was a lie. Selene wasn't resting at all—I just saw her stomp down a hallway. I opened my mouth to protest but thought better of it. Now wasn't the time. If I started calling out all the lies Simone had told me over the years, we'd be here forever, and I had a tour to get to.

"Happy to hear that Selene is well. And I'm glad I ran into you, because I have her notebook." As I pulled the binder out of my bag, I thought I saw a flash of panic cross her face.

"How kind of you to pick it up..." She seemed to want to say more but hesitated.

"My pleasure." I handed it to her.

"See you later," she said, taking a step away, then turning slowly back to face me. "Wait. How did you know it was my sister's notebook?"

"It was sitting on the table in front of her chair. At the panel."

"Of course." She chewed her lip ever so slightly. "Did you happen to read it? I'm sure that you are very interested in what she has to say about Isabella Dare. I'd be tempted myself if I stumbled across a competing scholar's work."

"No, I didn't read it," I said truthfully.

She examined my face. "Well, that's good because we're rivals in this award—"

"Simone," I said, shaking my head. "I didn't read it because there was nothing to read."

She froze, crumpled slightly, then rallied, forcing a laugh. "Oh, she must have brought the wrong notebook. How silly of her." She made a show of examining it briefly. "Ah, yes. This is just the one we use to draft things."

"You don't write on a computer?"

"No." She lifted her chin and stared straight into my eyes. "We decided to do it all longhand."

I knew that was a lie as well. Many a day I'd passed Simone in her office, tapping away on her computer. She also told anyone who would listen about the trials and tribulations of writing her book. I'd known that part. Everyone did.

I just hadn't known that her sister was writing half of it too...on the topic that I'd worked on for years.

I became aware of someone hovering beside us and turned my head.

The turquoise wrap Bibi Callahan had flung over one shoulder was lovely, if fuzzy, but I could practically feel Simone recoil—she had surely never worn anything homemade in her life.

"I loved your panel," Bibi said. "Hope that your sister has recovered?"

"She's fine, thank you." Her voice was colder than usual. "Would you please excuse me? I need to attend to her."

Bibi and I watched Simone sweep away with her head held high.

I couldn't explain to Bibi that Simone had been engaged in strenuous performance, pretending to tell the truth, so I just said, "I'm sorry about that."

"She must be very worried about her sister," Bibi said thoughtfully.

Sure. That's what it was.

"Well," Bibi said, taking a step closer. "I was fascinated by your excerpt. Do you have a few moments to chat?"

"I would love to, but I'm supposed to go on the tour—would you like to join me? I have an extra ticket."

"I can't, I'm afraid. I'm heading into another panel. But I think your writing is compelling, and I simply can't wait to read your book."

"Thank you. That means so much to me. Have you read Isabella Dare?"

"Oh, ages ago." She paused, when the turquoise shawl slid down her arm, tangling her up in it somehow. "Drat."

"I haven't met many people who have. May I?" I reached out and helped her straighten out the fabric.

She tied the ends together in the front. "There. That should hold it." She smiled at me. "I took up knitting after I retired. Still hoping to master it someday."

"I think you've managed to do so already. That's a beautiful piece."

"Thank *you*. And let's talk later? Really, I would love to hear more of your theories on the Dare books. My friend Pat wants to speak with you too." She twisted her head and shrugged. "Pat appears to have wandered off, but suffice it to say: she's a fan."

"That would be lovely."

Such are the moments that make conferences worthwhile. I would have been happy to sit and talk with Bibi and Pat all afternoon.

But now, I had a tour to attend. By myself, as it turned out.

And Lex was up there interrogating Flynn McMaster while I had to go look at a bunch of old props.

From where I stood, it seemed like detectives got to have all the fun.

Chapter 13

"Come this way, y'all," said Sunny, our aptly named tour guide, with a mega-watt smile. A middle-aged brunette dressed in yellow from head to toe, she was so perky that I couldn't imagine how she ever slowed down enough to sleep at night. Her smiles were cheery, her voice was bubbly, and when she moved, she even seemed to bounce.

We're talking supreme perk.

About twenty of us were making our way down the path to the barn. She pointed at the rusted water pump out front, which I hadn't even noticed was there.

"That's from the first-ever western shot here at Tattered Star Ranch: *The Range of a Cowboy's Heart*. Remember how they used it to fill up the buckets for the fire scene?"

Not waiting to see if we did, in fact, remember, she led us onward. We moved down main street past the shops that had also been built for *Cowboy's Heart*. They retained their original signage—we passed a saloon, barbershop, general store, apothecary, and sheriff's office, though we paused in the center so that Sunny could list the different films that had been shot on this spot, including a famous gunfight that had been spoofed so often even people who hadn't seen the original movie got the reference. She pointed out details like the hat still attached to an upper-story window by an arrow.

"I'm going to tell you a secret now." Sunny clasped her

hands together and beamed at us. "This whole row has been turned into one large gift shop! Please return later during your visit—we have everything from penny candy to posters—for all the souvenirs you could ever want honoring the many movies made here. Be sure to pick up something for all of your beloved friends and family members."

Once we reached the end of the row, Sunny led us through the cool, airy stables, where curious horses greeted us with soft whinnies from their stalls as we traipsed through the middle of their home. Tour members began taking pictures, posing for selfies with the equine residents. "Please don't touch," Sunny said sternly. "But do come back for our horse show held nightly."

I wasn't crazy about the way she kept promoting the things we could do here *other* than taking the tour, but I supposed that was to be expected. This was a business, after all. Tours made money. And I'd bought a ticket, I reminded myself, so I should try to get my money's worth. Sighing, I rolled my neck gently one way, then the other—I sensed a vague throb in my forehead despite the ibuprofen I'd taken—and vowed to be open to whatever came next.

We emerged in the harsh sunlight, near the edge of the forest that surrounded the ranch. When Sunny led us into the trees, I found myself at the end of the tour. Which was fine. I didn't want to make conversation, anyway. I trudged behind the others, listening to their exchanges. Everyone seemed to be having a grand time except me.

We arrived first at a clearing, which had been the location of several battle scenes in multiple westerns, according to Sunny, then continued deeper into the woods. The dirt path twisted often, and before long, I'd lost sense of which direction we were heading. It was difficult to see too far in the distance on either side between branches. The thick boughs above blocked the sunlight from reaching us, and the temperature dropped as the darkness increased.

Conversations gradually halted. This cathedral of green demanded silence.

We went on like that for I didn't know how long. It was picturesque but increasingly eerie. The air seemed charged with menace.

The further we went, the more my apprehension grew. I tried to sort out why. Was I hallucinating because of my head wound? Had I read too many fairy tales where dangerous things lurked in the woods? Or was my intuition legitimately trying to warn me about something? Whatever the source, I had the distinct feeling that someone was watching us.

Then Sunny took a sharp right, and we spilled back into the magnificent sun. "Are y'all interested in the horror films that were shot on the ranch? If so, here's one for you." Sunny's smile got even wider. "Any fans of *Monsters at the Slaughterhouse*?"

Some people clapped, and there were a few loud whistles from the back of the group. Banter broke out again amid a tangible attitude of renewal. Apparently I wasn't the only one who felt a sort of disconcerting spell cast by the forest.

Ahead of us loomed the dilapidated building from which people spent most of the film trying to escape. I was hardly in the right mindset to give this a try, but at least we were out of the trees. Sunny slid open a large door on tracks and motioned for us to follow her. The area was dark and full of shadows.

Large silver hooks hung from the ceiling, swaying slightly, over a cement maze on the right. A deep pit yawned on the left. Around the edges of the space were individual cells with metal doors. All three zones were sites of suffering for the characters. Seeing the space prompted disconcerting memories of the way killers in the film had slid noiselessly up to their victims and pounced.

As people headed over to the maze, enthusiastically trading favorite scenes from the film with their companions, I wandered off. Normally, I was interested in behind-the-scenes anything. I taught gothic literature and watched horror movies and had been looking forward to this tour for weeks. It would have been different if Lex were here. Alone, though, it was disturbing. My nerves had been on overload since Ellis had been found, and I realized that I just wasn't in the mood for horror right now. In fact, I was a bit freaked out by all of it.

So I aimed for the exit. I wasn't thrilled to be heading back into the forest, either, but the atmosphere in here was worse. As I approached the open back door, I heard a muffled shout and something that sounded like a thump. Distance to the source was difficult to gauge. When I peered quickly outside, I didn't see anyone, so I went over to the walk-in freezer on the side wall, which was the only other room on this side of the building. In the movie, several people had met their demise there.

I put my ear against the silver door but couldn't hear anything. If someone was trapped inside, however, I didn't want them to meet the same fate as the characters in the film. Grabbing the handle, I pulled. With a loud click and a whooshing sound, the door swung toward me. I was almost afraid to look, but I made myself do it anyway.

The interior was empty.

Relieved, I let go of the handle and took a step inside, just to check the corners that weren't fully visible from where I stood. A hard blow against my back propelled me forward and the door slammed shut behind me. I crashed onto the cement floor, white hot pain shooting through my palms and knees.

After bending my wrists and legs to make sure nothing was broken, I clambered back upright.

Did someone shove me in here intentionally? Now I was freaked out *and* mad.

I ran back over the door to open it, but there was no latch. Seriously? Who doesn't put a latch inside a freezer?

Oh, wait. Horror movie freezers don't have latches because if they did, the characters could stroll right out again instead of staying inside and freezing to death like they're supposed to.

The cold air already felt like it was piercing my bones. Shivering, I pulled out my cell phone and checked for service.

None. Nada. Zip.

Should have expected that—the walls were as thick as a cave. I shot a glance around the freezer's dingy white walls, dirty metal shelves, and unidentifiable stains. I didn't even want to hazard a guess as to what those were.

Again, I pounded on the door, but no one came to let me out. Sinking onto the floor, I tried to come up with a way to escape.

Instead, my brain started doing Panic Math, calculating how much oxygen was in here and how much time I had left until it ran out.

Not that I know how to calculate *any* of that.

But my thoughts were scrabbling about, trying to find something to glom onto, and math is where they went.

I closed my eyes and did a round of diaphragmatic breaths to calm down, which was working nicely until it occurred to me that maybe I was using up the oxygen faster.

I shoved that idea away and started another round of breaths.

Suddenly, the door was open—blessedly open—and Sunny was poking her head inside. "Hello there! Are you okay? What happened?"

"The door closed on me."

"Aw, you're not the only one, sweetie. All of the tour guides have found a Freezer Victim—that's what we call y'all, no offense—at some point. Dang door weighs more than my car does. That's why we have a protocol here at Tattered Star Ranch. I am required to check this location each and every time we are fixin' to leave the building."

"Thank you so much," I said, scrambling to pass her as she prattled on.

"And this is only the second time I've ever found someone inside...how exciting!" She put her free hand on her heart, delighted to have a new Freezer Victim anecdote to tell at her next tour guide meeting. "The *first* time was quite a shock—let's just say some honeymooners were celebratin' their nuptials. I don't think *they* would have minded if we'd left them in here all night!"

As she closed the freezer, I went directly outside and turned my face up to the sweet, sweet sun. Before too long, though, the heat intensified the throbbing in my head, so I edged into the shade. Sunny bopped over with a first-aid kit and helped me clean up the wounds. I was sore, but the scrapes would heal. When she warned me to be more careful, it was almost humorous. Between the microphone injury and the face plant and the freezer fall, I would be lucky to limp out of here alive.

Then I remembered that there was a killer on the loose and revised my thought: we all would be lucky to get out of here alive. If I wasn't helping with the investigation, I'd consider leaving right now. I pulled out my phone—happily working again now that I was outside of slaughterhouse walls—and texted Lex, asking how the conversation with Flynn had gone. He didn't answer. When the group had finished their exploration of the structure, we plodded back onto the dirt path—thankfully going in the opposite direction this time, away from what I could only think of as That Part Of The Forest Where Maybe There Are Eyes Watching You.

Sunny called over her shoulder. "If you look through the next patch of trees, you might be able to see the carnival set from the cult favorite, *Terror Along the Midway.* We'll get there in a bit, but first, we'll visit the graveyard where the souls of the Trail Way Gang are said to walk at night. You'll remember them from the classic western, *A Long Ride to Santa Fe.*"

Some applause and happy squeals burst out behind me. I rubbed my temples. I wanted this tour to be over with. I was tempted to ask Sunny for a shortcut back to the hotel, but I reminded myself again that the tickets had been expensive, and it seemed like a waste to give up now.

I glanced at my watch. Twenty minutes left. I could do this. Just walk, Lila.

Sunny pulled open a metal gate and gestured toward the headstones. "Feel free to wander. See if you can figure out which one is the intended grave of Stetson McAvoy, the hero of the film. Remember that they only got his plot half-dug-out before he came roaring back to life?"

As I was first in line, I aimed for a shady spot in the far back corner, which might help ease my headache. Others ambled around, but I moved with purpose: I needed to get out of the sun. I passed row after row of graves, barely glancing at the headstones.

When I reached the corner, I almost tripped over a wooden shovel handle resting beside a pile of dirt. That must be the grave Sunny meant.

I took a few steps closer, peering down into the hole.

At Flynn McMaster.

The next sound I heard was my own scream.

Chapter 14

An hour later, I was back in the hotel, waiting for Lex, who hadn't been interviewing our keynote speaker after all.

Obviously.

Lex had been en route when the hotel manager called with a potential lead that needed immediate attention. The next time the detective saw Flynn was in the cemetery.

At the scene, he had to help collect statements from everyone on the tour, but Lex had kindly talked to me first so I could leave. I'd returned to the room and collapsed on the bed. All I wanted to do was sleep and ease the pressure in my head. But whenever I closed my eyes, I relived what I'd seen in the grave: man, dirt, shovel. The latter had been bagged by crime scene investigators, but not before I observed something dark red on it. Someone had used that shovel on Flynn, I was sure. The shout and thump I'd heard before I ended up in the freezer—was that the murder in progress?

It was too awful. I couldn't believe he was gone.

Sitting up, I grabbed the book of essays from my nightstand—the *Go Ahead and Scream* title now carrying terrible resonance—and looked at the final section, which included pictures of Flynn at work in his office, pages of the manuscript covered with editing marks, and an overhead shot of his desk, which was cluttered. I studied them all closely. Nothing jumped out at me, but there was something about the last picture that tugged at my mind.

I squinted and brought the picture closer. Was that Selene's ring on the desk? What would that be doing there?

I pulled out my cell phone and snapped a picture of it to show Lex. Immediately after the snap, the phone trilled, sending me a mile into the air. It was going to be a long time before this jumpiness subsided.

"I have the list," Richmond said after I answered.

I was silent, trying to make sense of his words.

"You know, the list of scholars who submitted to the McMaster book?"

"Oh, thank you! Where are you? I'll come down."

We made plans to meet in the lobby by the main fountain. I didn't know if he'd heard about Flynn or not. Everyone on the tour knew what had happened, so word was likely to be getting around like wildfire, but if he hadn't yet been informed, I'd have to tell him.

The whole elevator ride down, I tried out different ways of bringing it up, but there wasn't a smooth way of delivering such news.

As I walked across the lobby, Acadia raced up and clutched my arm. "I need to speak to you." She pulled me into a nook behind a sunflower sculpture. "I heard...you found Flynn, right?"

I nodded.

She shook her head. "So sad. It's devastating."

"Absolutely tragic," I agreed.

Acadia craned her neck, checking to see if anyone was within earshot. Once she was satisfied that we were in a safe zone, she let go of my arm.

"People keep asking if we're going to cancel the rest of the conference. The police even suggested that we consider it. I've gone through this from every angle. It's quite conceivable, even likely, that the killer—"

"Or killers?" I blurted out. I mean, we didn't know how many were involved. Her eyes widened and she affirmed my point with a nod as she continued her sentence.

"—is here, among us. But I can't afford to cancel at this point. People have paid upfront. If we end it now, they'll ask for their money back, and I won't be able to pay the hotel bill."

"I see."

"But if we don't cancel, then the killer may strike again."

"That's true."

"But if we do cancel, the killer may strike again anyway."

I was trying to follow her logic when she went on. "You know what? Never mind. It's only a few more hours, right? And the Gala is the most anticipated event of the whole week. We have to keep going." She set her jaw and pulled herself up. "Thank you for the talk. I really needed to bounce it off of someone. Now I have my answer."

She marched across the lobby with visible resolve. I guessed she was heading toward a conversation with Chief Cortez or someone in a position of authority.

I followed, speeding up when I saw Richmond in one of the club chairs near the multi-tiered fountain. He was holding a sheet of paper and staring dejectedly into the water. I took the chair next to him and said hello.

"Lila, good to see you. Glad that you're still in one piece." He stopped short and stroked his chin. "That's not something I'd usually say to a person, but with people dropping like flies around here, perhaps you'll forgive me. Under the circumstances."

So he had heard already. News was orbiting the conference at light speed.

"I'm glad to see that you're doing well too, Richmond. And yes, we are in unusual circumstances."

He contemplated his shoes—one of the polished wingtips needed tying but he didn't seem inclined to remedy the situation—before replying. "Do you have any idea what's going on? What does your detective friend have to say?"

"We haven't been able to talk since...this afternoon," I said.

"Well, before that. Does he have anyone in his sights?"

"Maybe multiple suspects? I haven't heard of anyone in particular."

He made a harrumphing sound. "You'll forgive me again for my impatience, but it is making me very nervous that the people around me, in particular, appear to be targeted. Not that I was feeling very happy with Flynn, mind you. He's made a mess of things for us at the press, but I certainly wouldn't wish any bodily harm on him."

It seemed like an odd thing to say. I watched him closely. Was he telling the truth or playing defense?

A tear leaked out of the corner of his eye, and he stuck a finger behind the lens of his glasses to press on the lid. He cleared his throat, obviously struggling to gain control over his emotions. "Anyway, I hope that the police will find out who is behind this. I would leave early, but of course there's the matter of the award, which is supposed to be presented tonight. Which is its own problem. We didn't even get to the question part of the panel—" Richmond stopped short and shifted positions. "Never mind about that."

I went for broke. "Are you talking about Selene's manuscript?" I hadn't bought Simone's explanation, but I didn't know what was going on, either, generally speaking.

He glowered. "How—how do you know about that?"

"I found her notebook on the table after she fainted. Remember I tried to give it to you, and you asked me to return it to Selene instead?"

"Ah. So you're aware that there's an issue."

I hadn't shown Richmond or Candace the blank paper in the notebook, but he appeared to be informed. And we both understood what he meant by issue.

"Well, I saw those pages. Did she turn in a different manuscript to the judges?"

"I shouldn't talk to you about it."

"Of course." I blushed. "I'm sorry. I was just curious."

He held his breath, seeming to want to say more, but instead tightened his lips and pitched himself forward, out of the chair. "No need to apologize. I think we're all under quite a strain right about now. You just reminded me that I must find the judges and have a conversation, so thank you for that."

He handed me the page and bid me farewell for now.

The latest panels had just finished up, and the lobby was filling with scholars. He took a few steps ahead and disappeared into the crowd.

I scanned the list and noted only one person who was here at the conference: Beckett Thurber Standhouse, III.

As if summoned, the man himself strolled by a few feet away, holding hands with Selene. Today, he was wearing a blue suit with a red tie. She wore a dress in the exact same shade of red. I wondered if they'd planned it or if that was just how their life went: they were so perfectly suited that they matched without trying. Their hair was even the same shade of sun-kissed yellow.

Was it me, or was that a little too Stepford?

I needed to go tell Lex about the name on the list.

"Beckett Standhouse?"

"The third," I added, since Selene wasn't here to say it.

Lex pondered this. "He's the only one?"

"Yes. And the more I think about it, the more it might make

sense that he's part of the puzzle. Beckett has a book coming out on Flynn McMaster, which means he's an expert who has already been recognized by the press as such since they've given him a contract—"

"It must have been quite a slap in the face to be rejected from the critical guide project." Lex had picked up on my line of reasoning. "That would give him cause to be angry with the editors."

"Like Ellis." I paced across the room. "And he's close friends with Flynn too."

Lex's head shot up. "They went to grad school together."

"And now they work at Fairlake University in the same department." I stopped in front of the window and gazed at the sunset, all orange and red at the horizon with a curtain of blue pressing down from above. "Or they did."

We both were silent for a moment.

Lex cleared his throat. "We should ask your friend Nate if there's any history there."

"I can do that. Last night, they seemed fine, reliving their college days."

"Okay, so Dr. Standhouse has zoomed up the charts as someone who might actually wish to do Ellis harm." He paused. "But why target Ellis? What about the other people who work at the press?"

"Maybe he isn't the only target there. Maybe he's just the first one to be attacked."

Lex nodded.

"Though now there's Flynn as well, and he didn't work at the press."

"And we're back to Beckett having a friendship with Flynn." He wrote something in his trusty notepad.

"They genuinely seemed to care about each other."

Lex gave me a meaningful look. The kind that said I was far

too trusting.

"Those were the biggest bear hugs I've ever seen. And 'bro' was used many times."

"People don't always advertise their true feelings. You know that. Let's give Beckett a visit." He pulled a stack of papers out of the canvas field bag he used as a briefcase, explaining that he'd obtained a list of room numbers for all the conference attendees to make things easier. He scribbled Beckett's room number into his notepad and flipped the cover shut.

We went quickly to the room and knocked on the door. The TV was blaring inside. Lex made an exasperated sound and knocked louder.

"The food's here," Beckett was saying over his shoulder as he opened the door. He'd loosened his tie and rolled up the sleeves of his white button-down shirt. His jaw dropped when he saw us standing there.

Selene came up and draped her arm over him. "Hello," she purred at Lex. She was wearing a very elegant—and very short—silk robe that threatened to open with her next movement.

"Do you, uh, want to come inside?" Beckett took a step backwards, pulling Selene with him. She stumbled a little but caught her balance and drifted into the bathroom. I could only hope it was to add some additional layers of clothing.

"Thanks," Lex said briskly, moving forward. I followed. Selene smirked as she closed the door to the bathroom slowly, peering through the crack.

Creepy.

The room was a mess, with clothes strewn over the desk, sofa, loveseat, coffee table, and king-sized bed. It was as if their suitcases had simply exploded in there. Beckett windmilled around the room, grabbing items from seemingly everywhere at once, and piled them on the bed. He turned off the television and ran a hand through the hair that flopped over his brow.

"I'm sorry," he said. "We weren't expecting company."

"No problem. We won't take up too much of your time, Dr. Standhouse. We'd just like to go over a few questions."

"Sure, sure." Beckett perched awkwardly on the loveseat. He crossed his arms across his chest, then uncrossed them, then crossed them again. "Whatcha got for me?" His casual tone was at odds with his body language.

"How well did you know Ellis Gardner?"

"He's my colleague." His hand flew up to his mouth, and he looked stricken. "Was. Was my colleague."

"And you worked together with Flynn McMaster at Fairlake as well?"

"Yes. We are—were—all in the English department. Along with Candace and Richmond."

"And me, darling. Don't forget me. I also work there." Selene emerged from the bathroom, a cloying scent arriving as she did. She was still in the robe, I noted. So basically, she just ducked in there to put on perfume?

I wished I could assign demerits.

"Did you ever have any disagreements with Ellis?"

Beckett turned his head back and forth between us, then recoiled. "Wait, you don't think I had anything to do with his...his..."

"Death," Selene interjected calmly.

"We're not making any accusations at the present time," Lex said. "We're trying to gather information."

"The only thing Ellis and I ever argued about was the Oxford comma," Beckett said, adamantly. "Otherwise, we were fine, always."

Lex dipped his chin. "What about the book?"

Beckett had a blank look.

"The critical anthology," I clarified.

He didn't move. "I read it," he said slowly. "Not sure what

you're getting at."

"You submitted an abstract—"

"Oh! Right. But I didn't get in."

"Were you upset about that?"

"I was at first," Beckett said, his cheeks reddening.

"He was *mortified*," Selene chimed in, which only intensified Beckett's blush. That didn't seem like the most supportive thing she could have done, but he didn't seem to mind.

"Okay, yes. I was embarrassed. You could say that. But after a few days, I realized they'd probably excluded me because I had a book coming out with them and they didn't want to dilute my argument. You know, having it appear in both places."

Lex checked in with a glance, and I nodded. Made sense. Sort of.

"I got over it," Beckett mumbled. "And I wasn't mad at Ellis."

"Detective Archer," Selene laughed prettily, "you *already* know who is furious with Ellis. It's Flynn. He announced it to everyone at dinner last night."

Lex cut his eyes to her.

"They sent him a copy of the critical guide a week before the conference, as a courtesy, and as soon as he read it, he was enraged. I happened to pass by his office one day and overheard him complaining about the book to someone on the phone. Still, I never thought he'd turn his keynote address into...whatever *that* was." She smoothed her hair back, the diamond in her ring catching a sunbeam and producing a multicolored spot that slid over the walls with her movements. "Not that I think Flynn would ever hurt a fly. He doesn't believe in violence."

"He writes about it enough," Lex said.

She rolled her eyes. "But that's *literary*. Authors write all kinds of things that they don't do or think themselves, Detective

Archer. You know that."

"Mmm hmm." Lex didn't appear persuaded.

"Yeah, you should talk to Flynn," said Beckett, obviously relieved to be able to point a finger in another direction.

"We can't do that," Lex said slowly.

"Why not?" Beckett asked indignantly. He warmed to his theme. "Why is it only *me* you're talking to? I didn't do anything."

"Because he's gone," Lex said softly. "I'm sorry to report that—"

"Gone?" Selene repeated. "He left? Where did he go?"

The detective shook his head.

After a beat, they both seemed to understand simultaneously.

"He's dead?" Beckett gasped.

Selene gripped his shoulder as tears began to roll down her face. "What happened?"

"We're still trying to sort that out," Lex said.

"I'm so sorry for your loss," I said.

The two of them clasped each other and wept.

Which, Lex said later, was either raw grief or excellent acting.

This detective stuff had the potential to make one very cynical.

Chapter 15

"What do you think?" Lex strode down the hallway like a man on an urgent mission. Which, I guess, he was.

I increased my pace, attempting to keep up. "Was Selene trying to throw Flynn under the bus a little bit?"

"Maybe she was trying to get the focus off of her fiancé."

"That makes sense. Being loyal. Beckett did seem nervous."

"He did indeed."

I followed him through the fire door into the stairwell.

"But then again, there was that comment about Beckett being mortified when he didn't make it into the book, which gives him a crystal-clear motive. Wait. Lex, what if she was trying to redirect any focus from herself?"

"Why would you think she was angry at Ellis?"

"I don't. But there's something...*off* about her."

"Noted."

"I mean, she didn't race to put on any clothes when you came in. Just swanned around in the robe. Who does that?"

"I didn't notice."

I caught up to him and poked him in the side. "Liar."

He laughed.

"I think she was trying to distract us however she could." I threaded my arm through his. "Thanks for not looking."

"I only have eyes for you, Professor."

"You better."

*   *   *

In the room, we sat down on the sofa and compared notes.

"We have two lists now, Lex. One: people who were upset with Ellis. So far, the only ones we know of are Beckett and Flynn. But Flynn appears to have moved to the victim side of the list now. Which leaves us only with Beckett. Who did seem nervous. We agree on that."

"Correct."

"The second list focuses on those who were upset with Flynn. We know that the scholars walked out of the dinner last night, so they are clearly angry. One or more of them might have decided to take things into their own hands."

"I'd say so. I'll get someone to round them up again, stat." He punched a message into his phone.

"We already spoke to Richmond and Candace."

"Yes. And I interviewed Meredith and Hanover as well. Everyone at the conference connected to Fairlake—"

"Press or university?"

"Both. All such individuals have now been questioned."

I stared at him. "When did you do all that?"

"I continue flying solo when you're off doing professor things, Professor." He winked.

I allowed this to pass without remark. "Is there anyone else who might have had an issue with Flynn that we could add?"

Lex let out a small huff of air. "You mean aside from any number of fans or people with whom he worked on the films or other authors or colleagues? With someone who has achieved this level of celebrity, the list could go on and on."

"Good point." That was depressing. "But remember that I saw Selene coming out of his room this morning." It seemed like days ago.

He tapped his lip with his pencil. "You think they slept

together?"

"He did make a comment that strongly suggested that possibility." I paused. Sometimes the academic style of allowing for exceptions didn't work as well outside of academe. "Okay, yes. There really was no other way to interpret it."

I went over the whole encounter for him, adding as much detail as possible.

"Looks like I'll be asking Dr. Raleigh some additional questions."

"You know, that's probably why she was trying so hard to distract you," I said.

"That and my undeniable good looks," he said, elbowing me.

"That too," I agreed.

We added a few more names of people at the conference to question, like Acadia, who also had a run-in with Flynn. But they didn't have much of a connection with Ellis, as far as we could tell, so Lex expected to be crossing them off of the list promptly.

"I'll take care of those. It's always better to have too long than too short of a list," Lex said. "Is there anyone from the tour you think we should add? You *were* in the vicinity of the incident. Anyone who started out with the group but disappeared?"

"I don't think so. Though at one point I was...um...separated from the group."

"Why?"

"Long story." I didn't want to go into the whole freezer episode right now.

"Sorry, I didn't even ask about it. How was the tour?"

"Worst. Tour. Ever."

"Really? It's gotten so many rave reviews. What didn't you like?" He paused. "Before you got to the cemetery, I mean. I'm sorry. I know that was rough."

The mention of the cemetery brought everything rushing back. I swallowed hard, trying to push the image of Flynn in the grave out of my mind.

He put an arm around me and studied my face. "You okay, Lila?"

"Working on it."

Thanks to the other officers in the hotel, the contributors to the anthology had already been herded into the same room where we'd met before. This time, they were visibly uncomfortable.

Lex asked them where they were this afternoon, and all of them said they were at panels. He flicked his eyes to me, asking silently if it could be verified, and I shook my head. That would be difficult, if not impossible. Panelists were named in the program, of course, but no one in the audience signed in. Attendees could wander from panel to panel freely, even leaving one in the middle to join another one scheduled at the same time. It wasn't like a classroom where there was a roster.

"I heard about the keynote speech," he said. "And I understand you left the room together before the dinner was over."

He made eye contact with each scholar individually until Shanita exclaimed, "Wouldn't you have? I mean, he told everyone in our professional community that we don't know what we're doing! It was humiliating!"

They burst out with variations of what she had said, talking over one another, but agreeing on one thing: Flynn McMaster had ruined their lives.

Lex leaned back. I could practically see his idea inscribed in the air: we didn't just have one potential suspect here. We had five.

When the volume had subsided slightly, he spoke. "So to get back at him, you pulled some kind of *Murder on the Orient Express* scenario?"

They went silent, then the room overflowed with vehement denials that they had anything whatsoever to do with the professor's demise.

I'd let him sort through that. The panels were letting out soon and I needed to make some inquiries of my own.

I waited outside the panel that Nate and Calista had attended, "Symbolism in Gothic Poetry and Prose," which blended both of their areas of expertise. When they streamed out of the room with the rest of the audience, I led them over to the terrace behind the restaurant. It was between lunch and dinner, and most of the people at the hotel were hustling off to the final paper presentations of the day, so the tables and chairs were all empty.

"I know you're going to another panel soon, but I need to talk to you both."

"We heard about Flynn," Calista said. "Is it true that you found him?"

"Yes, but—"

"How many is that now?" Nate stared at me. "I don't know how you do it, find all the bodies in town."

"Not on purpose," I said, frowning at him.

"I know. But it seems to be one of your gifts."

"If so, it's a *terrible* gift. Anyway, can we please focus? I need to ask about your conversation with Beckett and Flynn last night. What did you talk about? Any sort of conflict?"

Nate drummed on the table as he thought back.

Calista took a drink from her water bottle.

A group of conference attendees drifted past the terrace. I

bet they were heading toward the graveyard. There was a sort of macabre fascination with crime scenes that often draws people to them.

"It was just hashing over old times," Nate finally said. "And catching up."

"Nothing seem tense between the two of them?"

He shook his head.

"Wait. What about the thing you said right before the panel?" Calista asked him. "About Flynn's idea?"

"Oh." Nate turned to me and lowered his voice, resting his arms on the table. "Beckett did say something—jokingly—about how Flynn had certainly made the most of The Idea. Capital 'T,' capital 'I.' It was very much emphasized."

"What do you think it meant?"

"I don't know. Hard to tell with all the teasing back and forth. You know, *Screw you, buddy. Back atcha, big guy.* Laughing while they said it. No big deal. But now that I think about it, Flynn got up afterwards and left the conversation— supposedly to say goodbye to someone but maybe he was mad about the subtext. None of it registered until after we heard about what happened to him today." He sighed. "It's unbelievable. We had a lot of great times together. He will be missed."

"I'm so sorry, Nate," I said.

"Me too." Calista told him.

He thanked us, his voice low.

Calista invited me to join them, but I declined. I had to find Lex. We made plans to meet up for the Gala, and I left them to their scholarly endeavors.

Veering into the line at the coffee shop to buy two waters, I pulled out my phone to text Lex.

A voice I recognized as Candace's carried past the person standing in line between us. "We're just forging ahead with this thing, then?"

"What else can we do?" Richmond rumbled back. "The whole conference is waiting for a winner. We're the judges. We have to make a decision."

Meredith said something unintelligible.

"No, I do appreciate your having invited me to be a judge. It's not about that. I just feel uncomfortable about the situation."

I gripped my phone tightly and peeked around the person in front of me. All three were conferring, their heads close together.

They were the judges all along? Why not say that upfront?

"If you insist that we continue, let's begin with the obvious: the Raleighs are ruled out, right?" Candace said, more audibly. "We don't have a choice because Selene didn't produce a manuscript. That's become clear. And she didn't participate in the panel, either."

"I don't know about that. It doesn't seem right, does it? Simone wrote her half of the book. She did the work. Why should she be penalized? And Selene fainted. That's hardly her fault." Richmond sniffed.

"I'm not convinced that she actually did faint," Meredith opined.

"I agree," Candace said. "And look, I know your families have been friends for ages, Richmond. You're in a tough spot, but—"

"Can't we judge the submission based on Simone's part?" His voice verged on whining.

"Selene didn't do *anything*," Meredith reminded him. "How could she be given an award for doing nothing? That's absurd."

"But since we are judging it on the proposal, not the

completed book, and since Simone read at the panel, fulfilling the competition requirements, it would be just as unfair to exclude *her*." Richmond cleared his throat. "And I think we can all agree that her writing is top-notch."

I marveled at how the Raleighs had gone from almost being kicked out of the competition to now apparently leading the rest of us, at least according to one of the judges. They certainly lived a charmed life.

"Richmond, you can't just award it to them because you like them best—" Candace began.

"It's not that."

"It's exactly that."

I couldn't stand to hear anymore, so I left, hoping they didn't see me slinking away.

Chapter 16

An academic conference is a thing of beauty. In theory.

Scholars come together to share their professional expertise, and there is a great deal of potential for the lively exchange of ideas and information. However, there's also a palpable undercurrent—via surreptitious glances at conference badges—of credential competition, an instantaneous passing of judgment on school status and rank achieved. And it can be stressful, exhausting, and overwhelming to be at your professional best at all times.

After sitting in endless panels or feeling summarized in an instant of badge scrutiny, it's no wonder that social activities are welcomed by conference attendees with the giddiness typically reserved for holidays involving gift-giving.

The biggest activity this weekend, predicted the conference planning committee members, would be the Gala awards banquet and dance. Attendees had been instructed to come as their favorite writer or literary character.

I wasn't sure how many of my colleagues were going all in, but I was ready—thanks to the wonderful thrift shop in Stonedale, I'd dressed in a slinky seventies halter dress with platform sandals to honor Isabella Dare. The only picture of her I'd ever seen was on the book flap, wearing something exactly like that. No one else would know who I was meant to be, but I didn't care. It was my own little tribute to my favorite author.

I picked up the light black wrap from the bed, threw it over my shoulders, and grabbed my bag. Calista and Nate were meeting me at the pre-Gala cocktail hour. I had never wanted a cocktail more.

In an effort to avoid running into anyone, I took the stairs and slipped out the exit door at the bottom. The platform sandals proved slightly unwieldly, so I was picking my way carefully down the stone path in the twilight, completely focused on the ground. So focused that I bumped into a couple in the middle of a kiss.

"Oh, I'm sorry—" I began, then stopped when I realized that I was looking at Lex.

With someone I didn't recognize.

She was about my height, with long dark hair pulled back into a braid that was coiled at the base of her neck. Her fitted jacket over dress pants and stiletto heels was chic and refined.

Her arms were wrapped around my boyfriend.

His arms were wrapped around her too.

Everything inside my body—to my core—turned to ice. I swerved around them and kept walking. My brain couldn't compute what I'd seen. I moved numbly toward the barn, even though I heard Lex calling my name.

Footsteps became louder. There was a light hand on my shoulder. I spun to face Lex, who was speaking, but it seemed muffled and nonsensical—as if his words were tumbling out in slow motion.

"Lila!" He peered into my face, his expression concerned. The world slid back into itself and his intention became crystal clear. "Let me explain."

"Don't bother." I said frostily.

"Please, just listen."

I turned to go, and he grabbed my arm.

"Take your hands off of me," I said, through clenched teeth.

"I have nothing to say to you."

"But—"

"Who is she?"

He closed his eyes. "My wife."

The frozen sensation was melted instantly by fury. I pulled away. "Don't you dare follow me, Lex."

I could hear him calling my name again but I didn't turn around. Tears blurred my vision as I ran into the barn. The Patsy Cline song playing on the speakers almost did me in, but it was loud and provided excellent cover when I stumbled over to a dark, unoccupied corner and wept. I put my arms on the table and lowered my head, letting it out. It was the whole enchilada: waves of tears, great sweeping gulps of breath, total body shudders.

When the storm subsided, I lifted my head. For a moment, I stared dully at the wall, wiping my eyes and sniffling. While I was trying to compose myself, I heard my cousin say my name.

"Hey, sweetie." Calista patted my back. "Ready for the Gala?"

I rotated enough that she could see my face. Her eyebrows shot up. "Oh, Lil. What is it? Are you hurt?"

Sniffling my way through it, I told her everything. At the end, she hugged me fiercely.

"He has a *wife*? Did he ever mention that before?"

I gave a get-serious look. "No. I wouldn't have dated him if I'd known he was married."

Calista shook her head. "There has to be more to it than that. He doesn't look like a cheater."

"What does a cheater look like?"

"Good point." She evaluated my face and tugged my arm. "Let's get you into the ladies' room and reapply your mascara. It's kind of running."

"I don't have any with me."

"I do." She patted the large purse slung over her shoulder. "Are you kidding? I've got a whole cosmetics counter in here. Anything you could ever want."

"So that's why you always look so perfect."

"Ha! Untrue. But it's not about perfection, anyway. I just like to play around. It's about self-expression."

"What does that say about me, then, since I don't really wear makeup? Oh. It says nothing, I guess. Literally."

"Aw, good. You made a joke. That's a start." As we walked, her eyes swept over my costume. "Love the halter dress. Who are you?"

"I'm Isabella Dare."

She threw her head back, laughing. "Of course you are."

I took in her off-the-shoulder gown and elaborate jewelry. "And you are..."

"Mary Shelley." She curtsied. "I even have a quill in my bag in case I want to accessorize."

"Or write another monster into being?"

"Exactly. To think that she created *Frankenstein* out of mere ink and—" Calista stopped short and pawed through her bag until she had dug up an envelope and pen. As I'd seen her do a million times, she scribbled a phrase on the paper.

"Poem idea?" I smiled at her.

"Yes. A good one, thanks." Once she had tossed the reminder back into her bag, we continued down the hallway and through a door, where we discovered a women's lounge with mirrors lining the walls. Velvet chairs were placed at even distances in front of the mirrors, along a long marble countertop.

"This is so fancy," she said gleefully. "Do you remember when the big department stores used to have rooms like this? Nowadays, you don't see them very many places. I'm feeling nostalgic."

"They do evoke a certain era."

"I'm sort of surprised to find one in a barn." She tipped my chin up with her hand and assessed the damage.

"Don't take this the wrong way, Lil, but I think we need to start over. Okay? Could you please go through there"—she pointed to a gilded swinging door—"and wash your face?"

She dug a small zippered bag out of her capacious purse and began setting up a row of jars and potions in front of her.

Having Calista give me directions was helping everything feel more normal. I stood up, took a deep breath, and pushed on the door. As I walked in, I caught sight of Candace and Selene, both of whom were standing in front of the sinks, facing each other and waving their arms around. As the door swung open, the tail end of a sentence hung on the air: "—I *know* what you did."

"Sorry," I said, starting to back out. I was stunned both by the sight of them and by the words.

They looked at each other and dropped their arms. The argument was concluded for the time being. They both pretended nothing unusual had happened.

"Come on in," said Selene, looking into the mirror and lightly touching her hair. "I was just leaving."

"Me too," Candace proclaimed.

They hurried out.

I washed my face quickly and patted it dry, then returned to Calista, sharing what I'd overheard.

"How very interesting," she said, handing me a tiny jar of face cream. "Start with this."

"What do you think they were talking about?"

"This afternoon, I heard Meredith telling Richmond and Candace that she didn't think Selene really fainted at the panel."

"Back up. Where was this?"

I gave her the replay of the whole coffee-shop conversation

and by the time I finished, she looked shocked. "Richmond wants to give the award to the Raleighs? That is completely unfair."

"Okay, but let's focus on the other part of that...Selene didn't write her half of the book. That's the thing that has me baffled. Why would she sign a contract but not write anything?"

"Fear of failure? Inability to produce?" Calista guessed, replacing the lid to the face cream. She regarded me thoughtfully. "Which reminds me, how is your mystery going, anyway?" She was one of a handful of people who knew I'd begun a novel.

"Wait, failure and inability remind you of my novel?"

"No," she laughed. "Just thinking about writing in general."

"I was talking about the Dare book. Which itself hasn't been easy."

"Writing is never easy."

"There were days where I almost walked away."

"But you didn't, Lil. You kept going."

"I kept going."

"Which is the secret, after all: persevere."

"It's so simple and yet so difficult."

"Indeed. And I'm thrilled about your academic book. But," she leaned forward and whispered, "you have to make time to honor your creative writing too. You've been dreaming about writing a novel ever since we were kids."

"You're right. But we're getting off track here. Can we please get back to the utter weirdness of Selene bringing a notebook to the panel that just had blank paper inside?"

"Bizarre." She gave me a bottle of foundation, which I refused, so she made a sound of exasperation and told me to sit still while she made me up. "Just for once. For the party. Think of it as part of your costume," she said.

I sighed and gave in while she went to work.

After a few minutes of her applying various things to my face, I spoke up. "Do you think she (a) was too busy to write it, (b) found it too difficult to write once she sat down to do it, or (c) never intended to write it in the first place?"

"Sit still," she instructed. "Stop ticking things off on your fingers. I can't draw a straight line while you're wiggling."

"Sorry," I said. "But I just can't figure it out and I'd rather focus on that problem than on my own problem, you know?"

"I do." She lowered the liner pen and looked directly into my eyes. "I'm so sorry about Lex. If he was cheating, he's not worthy and you're better off without him. If he wasn't, he'll make it clear to you very soon. In either case, you can't do anything about it right now, so please have some drinks with me and try not to think about him tonight, okay?"

I agreed. But he would be lingering in the back of my mind.

"Anyway, Nate is probably here by now, so let's go out there and find him." She finished what she was doing and turned my face gently toward the mirror. "What do you think?"

I gasped. Didn't recognize myself. My eyes were huge, my cheekbones were sharply defined, and my lips were rosy and very full.

"You look fabulous," Calista said. "You're going to be the belle of the ball."

"So not my goal."

"Still, you look amazing."

"Thank you for putting me together. You're the best cousin ever."

"I know."

She guided me outside to the bar. Nate was seated at the end, staring glumly into his drink. Calista tapped him on the shoulder, and he brightened up. "I thought you two were blowing me off. Or that I was missing some incredible party happening elsewhere. I was having major fear of missing out."

When he spun on the barstool, he took us in from head to toe, and his jaw dropped. "Wow. I mean...yeah, wow. Gorgeous, both of you."

His reaction sent a little shiver through me, much as I would never admit that.

We all explained who we were—he was going for H.P. Lovecraft in a dark suit. He'd slicked his hair back and looked unusually formal.

Except for the dangling purple tentacles where a pocket square would go.

"What are those?" I pointed.

He reached inside the pocket and revealed a small rubber octopus. "They're my monster legs."

"Touch of class," I said, smiling at him.

"Appropriately freaky," Calista added. "Now could you please conjure us up a couple of drinks, Mr. Lovecraft?"

He waved at the bartender, and before long we were seated at a table next to the stage, watching the hall fill with people. Half a glass of wine took the edge off more than I had expected it to. I rolled my shoulders one way and then the other.

"Lil, do you mind if I tell Nate?" Calista asked.

"No. As long as I don't have to say it."

She whispered in his ear while I resolutely looked the other way.

"Seriously?" I heard Nate say angrily.

I felt a tap on my back. He was shaking his head. "What an idiot. If you need anything...like I could kick his...well, he works out a lot, doesn't he...but I could throw a punch or something before he kicks *my*—"

I laughed. "Won't be necessary, but thank you."

Nate looked into my eyes and said softly, "Whatever you need."

I remembered that he'd just gone through a break up, so I

said, "Ditto, my friend."

We tipped our glasses toward each other. It seemed as if we had just promised something without saying any words. I wasn't sure what.

Best not to overthink it. He'd offered friendly support, and I needed that right now.

Before long, we'd been joined by Selene, Simone, and Beckett. The Raleighs were wearing white flowing gowns—very bridal—and Beckett had donned a tuxedo and top hat. All three, according to Selene, were courtesy of Henry James's ghost story, "The Romance of Certain Old Clothes."

"It was one of the few stories that featured two sisters," Selene said, smiling. "One of my favorites."

"One of his more Hawthornian tales," Nate replied happily. Anything Hawthornian made him happy.

I wondered if Simone had ever read the story, which doesn't exactly have a happy ending for the siblings—one of whom marries the other's husband. Was it an overt dig at her, something about getting married first? Or was it subconscious choice? It could have meant nothing at all, of course, but one of the side effects of being an English professor was a tendency to analyze everything, literature or not.

Richmond, who said he was attempting to channel Charles Dickens, also wore a hat with his long coat, and Candace, who said she hoped her gown paid proper homage to Louisa May Alcott, followed soon after. We exchanged compliments on costumes—except for Selene, who asked if I was going for a retro streetwalker look. Simone said the cuts on my hands added an authentically gritty quality.

The very people I'd snuck down a staircase to avoid were all gathered together here.

Oh joy.

Chapter 17

Small talk took us through most of the dinner.

"Are Meredith and Hanover coming?" I asked Richmond.

"She may join us later. She's not feeling very well."

"Sorry to hear that."

"And Hanover has been working around the clock on the whole...situation," he said, putting one finger over his lips to indicate that we were not to talk about it. "I urged him to join us, but he prefers the screen to the scene, generally speaking."

Beckett addressed Candace across the table, gesturing toward her dark blue gown. "Louisa May Alcott? Nineteenth-century literature isn't my specialty, but didn't she write *Little Women*?"

She smiled. "Indeed."

"Well, *that's* not very scary, is it?" Beckett laughed.

"Depends on whom you ask," Calista said under her breath. I knew she was thinking about gender roles.

Nate, who taught early American, stirred at my elbow but didn't say anything—though I could tell he wanted to.

"It's not Monster Night anymore, anyway," Calista addressed Beckett.

"But even if it *were* still Monster Night, Louisa wrote many things beyond that book," Candace said, clasping her hands in front of her. "Including gothic stories."

"*The Mysterious Key and What It Opened* is my favorite,"

Nate said.

"I love 'A Whisper in the Dark,'" I added.

Candace nodded her head in our direction, acknowledging our contributions.

"Cheers," Beckett raised his glass, "you learn something new every day, I guess."

"Yes, you do," Candace said. "You absolutely do." She stared at Selene. I wondered if they had finished their conversation or if the tension would continue to smolder throughout dinner.

"Agreed. I just learned, in fact," Selene announced suddenly, "that Fairlake won't be publishing our book."

More of a bonfire than a smolder, then.

Richmond's head snapped up and his mouth flopped a few times before he found purchase to form words. "Where did you hear *that*?"

"Meredith called me."

No wonder Meredith had opted out of the Gala. I wouldn't have wanted to face the Raleighs after that, either.

Simone's expression was wounded. "Why didn't you tell us?"

"Oh Simone, don't worry." Her sister laughed. "That's not true, anyway, right, Richie? We have a contract."

"Which you broke," Candace said icily. "By not writing anything."

"We gave you a manuscript," Selene said calmly, picking up her knife and cutting a miniscule bite of steak, which she popped into her mouth.

"We already talked about this—" Candace began.

"Do you really want to do this here?" Richmond inquired gently.

Selene shrugged. "Here or anywhere. I have nothing to hide."

Simone was far more hesitant but seemed to realize that the cat was out of the proverbial bag and was now rolling on the table. "Here is fine."

"The second half of your manuscript was...not submitted." Richmond said, surely attempting not to embarrass them.

"I told you before," Simone insisted, "that was merely a technical mix-up."

Selene looked at her sister as if trying to remember her alibi. "Uh...I brought the wrong notebook."

Simone touched her forearm once, lightly, and addressed the publisher. "We can send you the proper file once we get home."

Selene laughed again. Her champagne may have been going to her head.

"As you wish," Richmond said, spearing a broccoli floret. He seemed willing to take whatever the Raleighs said at face value.

I could have told him a few stories about why that wasn't the best idea.

Maybe I would, later.

Candace pointed a fork at the twins. "I think what Richmond means is that *if* we are able at some point to read *the whole thing*, and *if* we think it works, we will issue a new contract."

Selene didn't seem fazed at all by Candace's pointed reference to her failure to provide material.

"But we already have a contract—" Simone began again.

They all started talking at once. My head swiveled back and forth, trying to hear what each person was saying. Finally, Richmond held one hand up and they fell silent.

"I propose we complete this conversation after dinner."

Simone sat up straighter in her chair. "But we're in agreement that Meredith was confused, then." She threw a look at us, her Stonedale colleagues, and lifted her shoulders slightly. Clearly, she wanted us to hear that everything was fine and to perhaps join her in a this-business-is-crazy commiseration.

Candace shook her head. "Meredith is most definitely not confused. The contract you signed before is null and void."

"What do you have to say about it, anyway?" Selene demanded. "You're not our publisher."

Candace gave her a dirty look. "Actually, Richmond is bringing me on board as a senior editor."

"Wait—" Richmond held up one finger. "That has not been finalized, Candace." He repositioned the napkin on his lap, thinking. "As I just said, we will pause on everything and continue to work together to sort this out. Yes, that's how we'll proceed."

Now it was Candace's turn to gape. "But we decided—"

"That's enough," Richmond warned her. "We're done talking about this."

Simone and Selene glowed at Richmond from across the table.

Candace snapped her mouth shut and shoved her mashed potatoes around her plate angrily with her fork so hard that we heard the china scratch.

Luckily, the servers swept our plates out of reach soon afterwards. They made one more rotation, depositing dessert plates in front of us, upon which rested miniature chocolate cakes with a skull and crossbones design on top, garnished with berries. I could hear attendees snapping pictures. Social media would be flooded with images of the delectable offering within minutes.

We all dug in eagerly—except the twins, who were faced away from the table, whispering about something. They reached an agreement just about the same time as we had licked the last bit of delicious frosting from our forks.

"No need to continue this discussion. We're going to take our book to another publisher," Selene informed us.

Simone didn't make eye contact with anyone.

"It just makes more sense," Selene said. "There shouldn't be so much drama involved."

Funny, since they were the ones who stirred up the drama in the first place. The drama would certainly follow them wherever they went.

"Honey," Beckett said, "That seems a tad hasty. Why don't you think about it for a while?"

Selene, regal as a queen, fluttered her fingers. "We have made our decision."

Beckett spoke haltingly. "Wouldn't it be strange, though—your husband continuing to publish with them after you leave?"

"Not at all, my love," Selene assured him. "Because it's *our* choice to leave. You do whatever you like."

This was so illogical. Richmond had just shut down the termination of their contract. There was no reason to do this other than to serve some misguided sense of revenge for having been questioned.

"We *will* leave our proposal in the running for the award," Selene added. "That only seems fair, given what you've put us through."

What the publisher had put *them* through? They sure turned that around quickly. I wondered if they really believed themselves to have been wronged or if they were simply crafty that way.

Richmond's face reddened as he glowered at her. "This is unacceptable."

Selene shrugged. "It's done."

"How very ungrateful." He stood, threw his napkin down on the table, and walked away, shaking his head.

Simone's body language said that she was not on board for

whatever her sister's plan was.

Perhaps Selene knew that the book was likely to be rejected and was being proactive to avoid that. Maybe she simply couldn't handle being rejected.

Still, it was a mess.

Selene smoothed the tablecloth. "I'm relieved, actually. Now I can focus on the wedding full time."

"That's right, you're getting married soon." Candace smiled at Beckett. She was more relaxed—practically jubilant, in fact—now that the Raleighs had withdrawn their book. "Congratulations."

"Thank you," he said, "I'm the luckiest guy in the world." He threw an arm around Selene and planted a loud kiss on her cheek.

She looked down at her hands and emitted a small shriek. "Becks! My ring is gone!"

The twins jumped up and began looking. As Selene and Simone fluttered about, Beckett repeated what Selene had told us at the after-party—the ring was an heirloom, an irreplaceable one at that. He went over to Acadia, who was sitting nearby, and whispered in her ear. When he returned, I overheard him tell Selene that he'd offered to donate a hefty amount toward next year's conference if Acadia could ensure that the ring was found.

Soon, Acadia was onstage with Selene, who described the ring in detail, asking everyone to check near their chairs and tables. People complied with enthusiasm, even crawling on hands and knees to search. Eventually, Acadia took to the microphone again. "Could we please ask you to go back to the hotel and cover the floors and surfaces there? We'll reconvene for the award portion of the evening in an hour."

A raucous cheer rose up from across the room. Someone had just decided to spend that hour in the hotel bar, I bet.

"I'll go to the lobby," Simone said. "To supervise the

search." She paused and touched Beckett on the arm. "I'm so sorry about this."

"Thank you," he said, giving her an affectionate look.

Selene and Acadia stayed onstage, directing the efforts of the crowd.

I remembered the photo from the book that I snapped earlier and pulled out my cell phone. I showed it to Beckett. "Maybe a visual will help—isn't this her ring?"

He stared at it suspiciously. "Why do *you* have a picture of Selene's ring in your phone?"

It did seem odd, now that the ring was missing. I hurried to explain. "It's from the book."

"What book?" His forehead was all scrunched up in his confusion.

"The one about Flynn—"

"This picture is of *his* desk?" He stared out over the crowd, processing. Then his face went slack, and he roared Flynn's name. "That *bastard*!"

His response seemed much bigger than the situation warranted until I watched him stomp over to Selene and confront her. I couldn't hear what was said, but the narrative was clear, even from where I stood. She shook her head vigorously as he flailed his arms around, but, eventually, she looked down and nodded. He took a step backwards, then stumbled over to a nearby chair, where he put his head in his hands. She followed and bent down to speak, but after a few minutes, he waved her away. She ran through the front doors and out into the night.

Poor Beckett.

His shoulders were shaking as he cried. I slipped into the chair next to him and tentatively patted his back. "Can I get you anything?"

He dragged himself upright and wiped at his eyes. I offered

him a clean napkin roll from the table. He shook the silverware out of it and dabbed his face. After a forceful sniff, he looked at me. "I can't believe it. That man took everything else from me. Now she tells me that they had a little fling once?"

"That's what she said?"

"Yes. It happened years ago. Short-lived. Over." Unlikely, judging from the way Selene had skulked out of Flynn's hotel room with a colossal case of bedhead.

"But once is enough." He stared across the room. "She was the love of my life."

"I'm sorry, Beckett."

He accepted this with a soft bob of his head. "Here's the kicker. You know the books he wrote? The ones that made him millions and ensured him fans forever all over the globe? That could have been me too."

"What do you mean?"

"The basic concept was *our* idea."

"It was?"

"Yeah. In grad school, Flynn and I'd had a few beers one day, and we came with the general premise for the series. Joking around. Broad strokes. Then I suggested we actually write the books together someday." He twisted the napkin. "At first, he made fun of me, but when I confessed that I was serious, he said they were too *genre*. Sounded horrified. Told me I should focus on my own Great American Novel instead. I tried that and failed. Meanwhile, he wrote the series without me." He made a fist and hit the table.

I jumped.

"I don't know why I ever listened to him." His whole body wilted. "I thought he was my friend."

"Did you ever talk to him about it?"

"No. I mean, what was there to say?"

"Exactly what you just told me, that it was your concept

too."

"But he's the person who *wrote* the books. He did all the hard work. I didn't feel like I had a right to complain. After all, I'd only been there for the initial spark. Plus, I knew Flynn. He revised history in his head. Once he'd convinced himself of something, you couldn't persuade him otherwise. For him, I was no longer part of the Powell Block genesis story."

I nodded. "Was it hard to be colleagues, considering all that?"

"Yes. Especially since I was compelled to write literary criticism about his novels, even though I knew it was self-sabotage." Beckett sighed. "And, as if that weren't enough, did you know that he put us in the books as characters? I'm Ascot Fallingsworth, the absurd sidekick to Powell Block's clear-sighted hero. The punchline of every joke. Powell, as I think we both can easily see, is Flynn."

"Oh. No, I didn't realize that. Though Ascot is beloved in his own right—"

"For being delusional, though. He denies the existence of monsters again and again, despite all the evidence to the contrary."

I didn't want to point out that Flynn may have been on to something there, judging from what I'd seen of Beckett and Selene's relationship.

"Everyone loves cheering on Powell and laughing at Ascot." He threw down the napkin. "And obviously Serena Lovington is Selene."

"The romantic interest."

"Yes. I thought his depiction of her was admiration. Wishful thinking. But, as it turns out, it wasn't. And now I know that he didn't mind broadcasting his feelings for her to the world despite what it meant for me. While he mocked me as a sidekick at the same time."

"That's—"

"Horrible. I know. Flynn was a horrible person." Beckett let out a deep breath. "A monster, turns out. I always thought that I was the horrible one, because I was so jealous of my friend's success. But he *wasn't* my friend. And I don't have to admire him anymore." He reached a hand out and touched my forearm. "You're a good listener, Lila. Thank you. I had to tell someone. It's been eating me alive."

"You didn't talk to Selene about any of this?"

"Absolutely not."

"Why not?"

His face fell. "She already thinks she's settling, marrying me. That she could have done better."

"She told you that?"

"Not in so many words. But it's clear. I don't know why she didn't break up with me and just go for it. Him. Whatever."

"Beckett, sounds like Selene didn't love him."

"I doubt I could ever measure up to the glorious Dr. McMaster in her eyes. But it's kind of you to say." He brushed his hair off to the left. "I understand that all of this looks bad, as if Flynn sleeping with my fiancée wasn't enough motive to kill him. But Lila, I didn't. I swear. You believe me, don't you?"

"Mind if I join?" I glanced up to see Lex standing next to us. Something inside of me constricted.

"I was just leaving, actually." I pushed back my chair.

"Please stay," he said, softly.

I ignored him. "Beckett, will you please tell the detective everything you told me? It may turn out to be important."

Beckett nodded miserably, and I walked away.

Chapter 18

Back in the hotel lobby, it was mayhem. People were crawling around scrutinizing floor tiles, slithering under benches, shoving their hands into the fountain, moving potted plants, and generally getting in each other's ways. I went out onto the dark terrace, which had been cleared off in readiness for the next portion of the Gala—they were moving us out of the Red Barn Event Hall for the "Dance Beneath the Stars." The rustic metal lanterns on poles along the sides had not yet been illuminated, so I switched on my cell phone flashlight and swept the ground from side to side, looking for the ring. When I'd almost covered the whole area, my beam landed on a pair of white lace-up boots.

"Hello, Lila."

I raised the light to see Simone's face with parallel trails of smeared mascara on her cheeks. She put one hand up to block the brightness and sniffled into a tissue with the other. Her eyes were unfocused.

I turned off my phone. "Are you okay?"

"No," she said. "I'm not. I don't know what to do."

"What are you talking about?"

She downed the last bit of champagne from a slim flute and rested it on the iron railing. "I'm talking about Selene." She was slurring her words. "You heard all that at dinner, so you know what's going on. And you're the one who found her stupid empty notebook in the first place."

"I did, but I don't know what it means."

"Of course you don't. No one does. But I'm going to tell you." She kicked the ground with her heel. "What it means is this: Selene has a history of troubles. I've helped her as much as I can. We've always been able to keep it private before. But it's out in the open this time, and she doesn't even seem to care!"

"What kind of troubles?"

Simone spun her neck lanyard, causing her badge to flip backwards and forwards. "Concentrating. Behaving. Making choices. Controlling herself. Telling the truth."

The last thing—at the very least—seemed to run in the family.

"It's one reason my parents wanted her in Stonedale. I was supposed to keep an eye on her. But you got the job, so instead she ended up far away with none of us there to help her."

I didn't say anything. The lanterns along the sides began to glow, emitting a soft white light. Someone inside must have taken pity on us and turned them on.

"In the past, I've been able to do the work. Cover for her."

"In what ways?"

Simone flicked her slim wrist outward. "In *all* the ways. But this time, she made it impossible. Both the book and the chapter we were co-writing are dead in the water."

"Did you know Selene hadn't written anything?" I asked, as gently as I could. No sense in pretending I hadn't figured out what had happened.

"No!" Simone fiddled with her lanyard again. "She kept saying that it was coming along nicely. Her plan was that we'd slip away on Saturday, she'd give me the manuscript to read, and we'd have a long talk about it in person."

"But then they scheduled the awards panel on Saturday."

"Yes. Still, she said we'd go to a little bistro afterwards, where I could read it."

"But then she fainted instead at the end of our panel."

Simone laughed bitterly. "So convenient, no?"

Even Simone thought her sister had faked it.

She picked up the glass and peered at the empty bottom, then set it gently back down. "You know, Lila, during this time, I could have been finishing my *own* book. I wrote the proposal. I wrote the sample chapters. We were accepted based on the strength of *my* writing on Brontë. Yet I ended up without a contract. All because Selene dragged me down with her. And it's not the first time. She has been a burden to me her whole life!" She put her hand over her heart and looked down. "I've never admitted that aloud before. I can't believe I said that."

"I'm so sorry," I said. "Anything I can do?"

She lifted her head to meet my eyes. "Find me another champagne?"

"How about some coffee instead?"

Simone shook her head. "No. I need to forget all of this. And I need to speak to Beckett."

"Why?"

She drew herself up and spoke deliberately. "He was *my* fiancé first. Mine. I never would have treated him this way. She's gone too far."

I flashed back to our first year at Stonedale, the way I'd noticed a diamond on Simone's hand catch the light at a mentoring meeting, and gasped. No wonder Selene's ring seemed familiar. "It's the same ring?"

"Yes, and I *loved* that ring, Lila. Cherished it. She treats it like it's a costume piece. So careless." Her eyes narrowed. "Selene tricked him, you know. She pretended to be me and slept with him one winter break. Then she told him she was pregnant. He broke up with me and proposed to her out of a sense of duty. He's an honorable man. Then she told him she lost the baby, but..."

"There was no baby," I guessed.

"Correct."

"He stayed with her?"

"He feels protective of her." She swiped at her eyes again. "I literally threw myself at him during the square dance—right into his arms—to remind him of what we had. But there's no chance for us. He loves her now."

I thought back to seeing Selene embrace Beckett while we were busy promenading. Only it hadn't been Selene. It had been Simone.

Now the argument that had immediately followed made sense.

And I was surprised about Simone's behavior. I hadn't figured her for the kind of woman who would try and steal her sister's fiancé.

Well, steal him *back*.

Did that make it better? It was all very complicated.

"She's always acted this way," Simone went on. "My parents explained to me at a young age that I shouldn't blame her, that she can't help it. It's just how she's made, is how they put it. I had to be the strong one and look out for her, they said."

Wow. A lifetime of not only having to look the other way but also feeling responsible for your twin's bad behavior?

"And they made it clear that I'd need to take care of her. No matter what."

Make that responsible for her, period. That must have been so difficult.

"I am furious with her and...and...my whole family."

"What can I do to help?"

"Nothing," she said. "Except please keep this between us. I shouldn't have said anything. It's just...I *cannot* carry this around anymore. Not for one more minute."

I remembered with a jolt that Selene had made Simone her maid of honor. Talk about cruel. I wondered if Simone still truly loved Beckett.

Or if Selene even loved him at all.

Beckett didn't think so.

Simone continued. "She told me you saw her sneaking out of Flynn's room in the morning. Did you tell Becks?"

"No."

She nodded her approval. "Better that she tells him herself. Or maybe not tell him at all. I don't think he could handle any sort of infidelity."

"He already knows about Flynn. Not this weekend, but—"

With a gasp, Simone jumped to her feet. "Oh no. I have to go to him. How does he know?"

"When Selene lost her ring, I showed him a picture from the book, thinking it might be useful to post it online somewhere or at least show it around, so people knew what they were looking for. He took it to mean—"

"Flynn's desk? Oh Lila, how *could* you? He'll be heartbroken. He's not as strong as you and I are."

"I didn't know. I was just trying to help—"

But she was already gone, in a flurry of white silk.

On my way back to the barn, I started to get that conflicted feeling I had much of the time Simone spoke to me, which was an authentic desire to believe her competing with hard-won knowledge that most of the things she said were likely to be partially or completely untrue. Sometimes I forgot who she'd shown herself to be and trusted her again. Which usually didn't turn out very well. She had a tendency to shift behaviors right when I'd let down my guard.

Part of me was surprised that Simone had complained

about her sister, to me of all people. The other part of me wondered why. Was it due to the vast quantity of champagne she had apparently imbibed? Or was she desperate to unburden herself by telling someone—anyone—as she'd admitted? Or was she spinning lies for her own mysterious purposes? It was hard to know which side of the truth-o-meter she was on tonight.

But this conversation had felt authentic. I couldn't explain what was different about it. I believed her, though, I realized with shock.

Wrapped in my musings, I was halfway down the path before Lex darted toward me from the shadows.

I ignored the hand he held out to me and kept going.

Wait. I just hung out *on purpose* with Simone Freakin' Raleigh but didn't want to come within ten feet of my actual boyfriend. Everything was upside down.

"Lila, please." His voice broke, softening my resolve. I stopped moving while he caught up to me. "It wasn't what it looked like. Helena just returned from her job in London."

"That's her name? Helena?"

"Yes. And it's true that I hugged her, and she kissed me on the lips—"

"I saw that part," I said coldly. "Don't need the recap."

"—but she just did it out of habit."

"Out of *habit*?"

"Some people are kissers." He threw his hands up, exasperated, which irritated me further. He did not get to be the exasperated one here.

"Wow."

"Lila, we're separated. We haven't gotten divorced, but we aren't together. I'm with you."

"You didn't even mention her. Not once in all that time."

"Because Helena and I weren't together when we started seeing each other. And you and I were so off and on again...it never felt like the right time. I may have been afraid of what you'd say. I don't know. But it doesn't matter. We can sort it out right now."

I shook my head. "I can't."

I hadn't told him about the time my first love broke my heart by cheating on me. He'd walked out of a party with someone else in front of me—I still had nightmares about that moment where I couldn't speak or stop him. Tonight had brought up all of those complex feelings of rage, shame, and grief.

"It was innocent. I swear. I would never do anything to hurt you. Never, Lila. She planted one on me before I knew what was happening and then you bumped into us." He stared into my eyes, pleading. "We can go talk to her right now. She's still here."

"Why is she at the hotel in the first place?"

"She went looking for me at the station—"

"Why?"

"I told you. She just got back to the states and wanted to see me."

When I didn't reply, he hurriedly added, "We're still friends. But as I said, we're separated."

"Does *she* know that you're separated, Lex? Because it doesn't sound to me like she does."

"Come talk to her. She'll corroborate what I'm saying."

"Corroborate? This isn't one of your cases."

"I know. But Helena felt bad after I told her that you'd seen us and thought we were together."

"Oh, *Helena* felt bad. Well, then. By all means, let's make her feel better."

"You know that I feel terrible too."

"Be that as it may—"

"Lila, I love you. Don't throw this away."

"You...wait, did you just say that you *love* me?" Suddenly I didn't care so much about Helena.

"I did."

"You really do?"

He nodded, his blue eyes never moving from mine. "I do."

I paused and took stock of my feelings. It didn't take long. For better or for worse, I trusted this man. I believed what he was saying about Helena. And I wasn't going to let a misunderstanding ruin the first time he told me he loved me.

"That's good, Lex, because I love you too," I whispered. "Though this is a heck of a time to have told me. Couldn't you have waited until we weren't in the middle of a fight?"

"No. I couldn't wait any longer. It needed to be said. And we never seem to do anything the normal way, Lila. Haven't you noticed that yet?" He took my hand.

"I have indeed. No more secrets, though. I mean it."

"No more secrets. I promise."

Some kissing followed. It seemed important to commemorate the exchange of such feelings with solid action.

Which was followed by some talking.

And a bit more kissing.

By the time he pulled out a tube of lip balm to replenish moisture balance, we were back on track, relationship-wise.

Or maybe even a little bit ahead. He'd told me all about Helena and their youthful but short-lived marriage. I'd shared a few things too.

As we walked back to the barn, I recounted the conversation with Simone.

He listened carefully.

"Do you think Selene may be dangerous, Lex? Do you think she killed Flynn?"

"She has been doing some strange things. No question about that. But why would she kill him?"

"Maybe she fell in love with him, told him she wanted more from the relationship, and he refused. Judging from dinner tonight—"

"What happened?"

"I'll fill you in on that later, but the point I'm trying to make is that I don't think she's someone who can handle rejection well."

Lex nodded. "Do we know for sure that it was in fact a relationship between Selene and Flynn, not just a one-night stand?"

"I don't know, but the picture of the ring on his desk is what set Beckett off. She convinced him they'd had a short fling that had been over for a long time." I paused. "I didn't mention the sleepover on Friday night. It doesn't seem like something I should report to him, you know?"

"Hmmm. I still think he has more motive than anyone else." Lex pulled out his phone. "I think we need to bring him in. But first...we're good, right? You and me?"

"Yes, Detective. I'd even say better than good."

He made arrangements while we continued down the path, and I had an idea. As he continued his conversation, I pointed to the hotel. He nodded to indicate that he understood and I sprinted—well, hobbled since the platform shoes were getting more uncomfortable by the second—to the registration desk.

"Hello! May I help you?" A round-faced man greeted me cheerfully. He had a mop of red curls and was dressed in a bright green tunic and hose instead of the somber hotel attire I'd seen on everyone else at the desk. Didn't know if he was channeling a character in the spirit of the Gala or if it was how he dressed all the time.

"Hello—"

"Mickey," he interjected, pointing to his nametag.

"Mickey. Do you have a lost-and-found?"

He reached under the counter and felt around, then pulled out a box triumphantly. "What are you looking for?"

"A ring." I pulled up the photo on my cell and showed it to him. He gave it a long stare, as if he were memorizing the shape, then set down the phone.

"Let's see what we have." As he scrabbled through the box and removed the items, I was somewhat surprised to see what emerged.

A necklace made of plastic teeth.

A threadbare wash cloth.

A canvas sneaker with frayed laces.

A polka-dotted raccoon toy with one eye.

A flashlight that did not turn on when Mickey clicked the button.

A half-roll of breath mints.

A key chain with a unicorn on it, devoid of keys.

And a plastic purple octopus.

"Oh, I know who that one belongs to," I said, making a grab for the octopus. I'd give it to Nate later.

"Alas, no ring." Mickey said sadly. "You're, like, the twentieth person to ask me to look for that tonight."

"Why didn't you tell me you'd already looked?" We could have saved ourselves some time.

"I hoped we would find the ring inside. You see, this box is enchanted. Sometimes you look inside twice and don't see something, but then the third time—poof!—it's there." He eyed the interior, as if trying to discern the mechanism that made that happen.

"Maybe someone turns the found item in before you check. You know, in between your shifts."

He stared at me. It was obvious that it was first time he'd considered the possibility that something other than enchantment was responsible for the appearance of objects in the box.

Though he didn't entertain the theory for long.

"Nah. It's magic." Mickey snatched the box from me and tucked it carefully back in its spot, giving it a little pat.

"Thank you for your help."

"Sure thing. Always happy to look inside the enchanted box. I've seen a lot of things you wouldn't *believe* working at this desk." He wiggled his eyebrows. "Trust me."

Well, that just got weird.

Chapter 19

The sounds of a commotion drew me to the front of the lobby. Through the glass wall, I could see that a large crowd had filled up the hotel parking lot. News trucks aimed bright spotlights at the proceedings and reporters were busily talking into their microphones. There was a line of police officers spanning the front of the building, facing the crowd.

I cupped my hands and pressed my face closer to the glass in order to see better. People held signs with quotes from Flynn's books. They were singing one of the songs from the first film. A pile of flowers and candles had been deposited near the door. Clearly, the fans had arrived to express their grief. I hoped that things remained calm and never entered any sort of hysteria threshold.

I scurried back down to the barn, where most people had reclaimed their seats, eager to continue with the Gala. I hoped Lex would join us on the terrace later when the dancing started. Too bad he'd missed the square dance, which had been more fun than I'd expected. Nate was an enthusiastic partner and had made me laugh. Then again, he always made me laugh.

On the way into the event hall, I swerved into the women's lounge, which was empty. Having touched some of the lost and found objects, I wanted to give my hands a good scrub. The confrontation with Lex—while upsetting at first—had cleared the air, and I felt lighter than I had in a very long time. I hummed a little.

While I was drying my hands on a paper towel, the door swung open a crack. Candace was talking on the phone and pushing open the door as she moved very slowly. "No, no. That's not true. Not at all. Seriously? Who told you that?" She listened, then made a sound of frustration. "An email? Robert, ignore it. I'm telling you, that woman is insane. I'll explain everything to you when I get home." There was a pause. "Love you too. See you Sunday."

She clicked off and came in the rest of the way, shoving her phone into her bag as she approached. When she lifted her head and saw me, she released a little scream.

I apologized.

"No need." She put her hand on her chest. "Just give me a sec."

After she'd slowed her breathing, she smiled at me. "Sorry about that. And, while I've got you—sorry as well about all that unpleasantness at dinner."

"It's fine. Hope that everything has been sorted out with the Raleighs."

She rolled her eyes. "The saga continues. As it always does with them. But I hope it didn't ruin your evening."

"Not at all. And congratulations on the new position at the press. Editor, right?"

"Yes." She smiled broadly. "Richmond made me an offer I couldn't refuse. Like he does."

"That's great news." I wondered if Simone could approach Candace as a single author. If her chapters were as good as she thought they were. Maybe I'd mention it.

"Thank you, Lila. See you back at the table in a few." She moved into one of the stalls and locked the door.

I went outside, where I spied Calista on the other side of the barn, waving. It took a while to cross over through the crowd, but when I finally reached her, she clutched my hand. "Did anyone find the ring?"

"I don't know. They didn't announce anything yet."

"Hey, at least we all tried. But now...it's awards time. Are you ready for this?"

"Cal, I don't even think the awards are happening."

"We'll see. Why don't you go back and save our chairs, and I'll bring you some wine."

I returned to our dinner table, which was populated with the same individuals from before. Beckett, I was surprised to note, was seated next to Selene, who had her arm draped over his shoulder. She must have convinced him to give her another chance. It was hard to believe that was the same man who had been crying just over an hour ago. He looked perfectly content.

They were already deep in conversation, so I sat down quietly.

"I respect you, Beckett." Candace had beaten me back while I fought my way through the crowd over to Calista. "You're an excellent colleague, and I know you care about your reputation."

He smiled humbly.

"So I have to ask: has Selene told you about her adventures this weekend?"

"Her award nomination?" Beckett smiled expectantly at Candace, eager to celebrate his fiancée's latest accomplishments. "Yes. Very proud of her."

"It's not your place," Selene murmured, but Candace's lips were already moving.

"No. I mean her adventures with Flynn." She rested her fists on the table.

Beckett's smile faded slowly. My heart hurt for him. He turned to his fiancée and shook his head. "Is it true, Selene? This weekend too?"

"It's not true," Selene said. "As I told you, that was over a long time ago. The photo Lila showed you doesn't mean anything."

He shot a glance at me. I felt terrible. Even if the photo wasn't evidence of anything untoward, I knew it had upset him.

I also knew that I'd seen Selene walking out of Flynn's room yesterday. Which would upset him far more.

And that shark seemed to be circling.

Selene went on. "You know how the ring is so heavy it hurts my finger?"

"You do mention that."

"Well, a few of us were in Flynn's office for a meeting, and I needed a break. Then I forgot to take the ring with me. It was only out of my sight for a little while. But someone obviously took a picture of his desk before I came back to get it."

Beckett's face turned hopeful. "That's all it was, then?"

"Yes, my love." She squeezed his hand. "I swear."

"Then how do you explain this?" Candace turned her right hand up and uncurled her fingers to reveal Selene's ring.

"Where did you get that?" Selene snatched for it.

"In Flynn's bedroom," Candace smirked. "Here at the hotel."

"What?" Beckett jumped to his feet. "Here?"

Selene jumped to hers too, protesting loudly that it wasn't what it looked like. They both yelled and waved their hands and didn't seem to be getting very far.

"I fell asleep in his suite," she screamed. "We didn't *do* anything."

"You did too. You lie!" Candace raised her voice as well.

Selene whipped her head around. "Will you just shut *up,* you nasty *cow*?"

"I will not. Flynn told me everything." Candace focused a laser beam of hostility in Selene's direction and began ticking items off on her fingers. "He told me that you'd been having an

affair for *years*. He told me that he was in love with you. And,"
she finished triumphantly, "he told me that your engagement to
Beckett was the worst thing that had ever happened to him."

"What were *you* doing in Flynn's bedroom?" Selene
demanded. "Care to explain that?"

"We're friends," Candace said. "He wanted a place to talk
quietly. You know how many people follow him all the time.
After he told me everything, I found the ring next to the bed on
the floor."

"Years? You've been having an affair for years?" Beckett
glared at Selene. "That's not what you told me earlier."

"I'm telling you, it's not true," she wailed. "Becks, sweetie,
let's go somewhere quiet and talk this out."

"No need. We're done." Beckett stormed away.

Selene stared daggers at Candace. "Why do you hate me so
much?"

Candace threw up her hands. "It's not about hating you,
though I will admit that I do find it difficult to *like* you. I'm
calling out the fact that you ruined your sister's chances for
publication and you ruined Beckett's life. And Flynn's life. And
what's worse, you don't even care."

"I care...I do...I..." Selene looked to her twin for support,
but Simone remained silent.

Selene sat down heavily in her chair.

Soon her head rotated slowly back in Candace's direction.
"Anyway, you're a fine one to talk. Everyone knows you were
having an affair with Ellis Gardner."

"No, I wasn't." Candace swatted that idea away. "Nice try.
And I know you emailed my husband with that ridiculous
rumor. Who does that? What is *wrong* with you?"

Selene mumbled something under her breath.

"What was that?" Candace asked, eyes pinned on Selene.

"I *said*: it takes one to know one."

Candace shook her head and walked to the other side of the room, where Richmond was speaking animatedly with Acadia.

I went outside looking for Beckett.

He was already being led by Lex to a police car parked behind the hotel—away from the enormous crowd building an impromptu memorial out front. Once Beckett was safely tucked inside, the driver pulled away.

I stared after him.

Lex came over to me. "It was necessary, Lila. We need answers from him."

"Thank you for being discreet. But I think you have the wrong guy. He didn't even find out about the affair until *after* Flynn was dead."

"Or he may have found out a long time ago and was playing up the innocent spouse routine."

I'd forgotten about that possibility.

"And you said he was angry about Flynn running with their idea." Lex replied. "He had more than one motive."

"True. But he just doesn't seem like—"

"Lila. We can't go on feelings alone in this job."

"That's not true," I retorted. "You listen to your intuition all the time."

He acknowledged this with a bob of the head one way, then another. "Maybe so. But you're forgetting that we *also* know Beckett Standhouse was very upset with Ellis. For excluding him from the book project."

"He said he was *at first*. But that he'd gotten over it. Which is completely normal. It's hard to be rejected."

"But maybe he's not really over it, Professor."

"Fair enough. Still, I would be very surprised if Beckett Standhouse was capable of killing."

"I appreciate your assessment, but we need to question him further, right now." He softened his tone. "Thanks for your help with everything. Not sure I've said that enough."

"All right, but will you please be gentle with him?"

"We will."

"What about Selene as a suspect?" I had to throw that out there.

"You did bring her up before. But why would she have killed Ellis?"

I shrugged. "Maybe there are two killers."

He blew out a puff of air. "You're right. That's always worth exploring. But that explanation is more complicated. Often times, the simpler answer is the right one. For now, we're looking for someone who had cause to attack both victims."

"I see."

"I'll keep it in mind though." After he'd taken a few steps, he spoke over his shoulder. "And don't go getting yourself into any situations trying to prove me wrong, okay? Stay safe."

I waved at him. "I won't."

I would do my best, anyway.

Not long afterwards, I was back at the table. Calista and Nate had both arrived. People walked between tables, laughing and snapping pictures together. Selene and Simone appeared to be deep in snub-your-sibling mode—looking anywhere except at each other. Beckett's chair was conspicuously empty. Richmond, by the wall talking with Acadia, waved at the Raleighs to come over. They stood and moved in his direction. Candace, catching sight of the twins moving away, quickly followed. She probably wanted to run interference in case Richmond got it in his head to offer them a new contract.

"Where's Beckett?" Calista asked, gesturing toward his

chair. "Isn't he up for an award? Not that I think he'll win—my money's on you, Lil—but wouldn't you think he would want to be here?"

"If I were him, I wouldn't," Nate said. "Poor guy. I don't care what Selene says—she was a big cheater. That's obvious." Under his breath, he added, "Little bit of Rappaccini's daughter about her, isn't there?"

I replied quietly in kind. "You mean she's poisonous, like in the Hawthorne story?"

"Through and through, from what I've seen. Who says Hawthorne isn't relevant these days?"

As much as I loved a good literary allusion, I needed to steer us back on track. "Beckett has been taken to the police station," I told them. "But keep it on the down low."

"Did Lex say what the plan was?" Nate asked. "Oh wait, you two aren't talking."

"Actually, we are. We had a long talk. He and his wife are separated. I misunderstood."

"Are you sure?" Nate crossed his arms, looking disappointed. "I mean, he could just be saying what you want to hear."

Calista considered what Nate had said. "What proof do you have?"

"I don't need proof. How could you even prove something like that?"

Their eyes met. They didn't believe me.

"Did you speak to her?" Calista pressed. "I mean, that would lend weight to his claims."

"He offered that, but I passed. Why would I want to talk to his wife? Trust me, I know Lex. He's telling the truth."

"Why aren't they divorced?"

"It's in the works."

"Why didn't they do it before?"

"They wanted to be sure. And she was overseas...and..." It felt incredibly strange defending my not-divorced boyfriend whom I'd just learned was married, so I stopped talking.

My cousin spoke, after it became clear that I wasn't going to finish the sentence. "I like the guy, and I want you to be happy."

"I want you to be happy too," Nate echoed.

"Thank you for that—and for helping me through everything before, when I wasn't sure what was going on."

We were quiet for a spell after that. I gave them a chance to process the news.

Simone returned to the table, her expression stony.

"Everything okay?" Calista smiled at her.

"Yes. I wasn't needed," Simone said airily, brushing something off of her sleeve. Her tone didn't match her drawn facial expression.

"What's going on over there?" Nate leaned forward. "I thought you and your sister did everything together."

"We don't, first of all." She attempted to cast a dazzling smile at him but it was wooden at best. "And secondly, I wouldn't know. They said they didn't need me." She turned away from us and pulled out her phone.

The subject was closed.

I peeked around Nate's back at the place where they'd been standing, but the trio was moving up the stairs, behind the curtain of the stage.

Well, I guess we knew who the winner of the award would be.

But why wouldn't Simone join them too?

Now that I thought about it, wouldn't Simone be the more appropriate person up there? She's the only one who did any writing.

I had no idea what was going on.

Acadia still hadn't gone up on the stage.

I took the opportunity to do a little more digging. "Hey, Simone, what was Selene saying about Ellis?"

She shrugged.

Here I thought we'd bonded earlier tonight on the terrace, when I'd offered a shoulder to cry on and found myself buried under an avalanche of issues. Big stuff. Heavy stuff. Stuff you would only tell a close friend.

Or therapist.

And now she was giving me the cold shoulder?

Did she not remember telling me? Or did she regret telling me? Or was she just drunk? I didn't know what her behavior meant.

It probably would have been easier to accept the fact that I would never be able predict what the Raleighs would do. At all.

But I couldn't, somehow.

"Simone, anything she has mentioned about Ellis might be important. Think carefully, please. Did she ever talk to you about him?"

"Not much. Just...basic colleague stories."

Those could certainly run the gamut from admiring to scathing. "No quarrels with him that you remember? Or with anyone?"

"Not until tonight. I mean, you saw the way Candace treated her."

"They both seemed to be giving as well as getting."

Simone blinked at that.

"What was she saying about Candace and Ellis again?"

"She said there were rumors that they had been having an affair for a long time."

Candace had literally laughed in Selene's face when that was raised. I wasn't putting much stock in that rumor, but you never know. "How about Flynn? Did Selene ever talk about him?"

"Why do you keep asking questions about my sister? Wasn't your interrogation out on the terrace enough?"

"Interrogation? There was no interrogation. I was just listening—"

"Yes, you did. You grilled me. You were insistent. You had to know all our private business, didn't you?"

"No, I—"

"Why can't you just leave us alone, Lila?"

"Leave *you* alone? You're the ones who proposed a book on a topic that you knew I was working on! You're the ones who asked if your book could be published ahead of mine while I was sitting right there! And you, Simone, are also the one who has relentlessly mocked me, my family, and every single project I've done—yet you've taken credit when you haven't lifted a finger."

She blinked again, rapidly this time.

"It's true," I said. "And you're a bully. But you always claim to be the victim."

"You do," Calista added.

"She's right," Nate said.

I leaned toward Simone. "Listen closely: you need to stop. Stop it right now."

She drew back abruptly. "I will not sit here and take one more minute of this attack." Simone scooped up her purse and shook her finger at me. "You are awful."

"See? There you go again." I pointed at her. "Whenever someone stands up to you, you flip the script. Make yourself into the victim. It's ridiculous, Simone. Enough already."

Her eyes widened, then she spun and marched herself to the back of the room to sit on a barstool.

Direct confrontation wasn't my favorite thing. I took stock and realized that I was shaking. It wasn't that I was scared, but sometimes when I had to deal with something emotionally intense, my body thought it was time to shoot out lively streams of adrenaline, as if decorating for a party.

"Good for you," my cousin said. "Brava."

"I concur," Nate said, looking down at my trembling hands. "But shall I get you a shot of tequila or something?"

"That's the last thing I need," I assured him.

"Let's just rest for a minute," Calista said. "Who cares who was having an affair with whom. We're here for the awards and..." she raised her glass, "the drinks!"

The jolt of energy seemed to be helping me think more clearly, make connections.

And then something clicked.

Something that had been right there all along.

"I've got to go," I said, jumping up from my chair so fast that it shot backwards.

Calista and Nate exchanged a glance.

"I need to move around anyway, release some of this extra energy." I shook my hands a little bit, which helped, then I picked up my chair and set it gently in place.

"Are you sure?" Calista looked concerned.

"Yes. Be right back." I moved quickly through the crowd before they could stop me. Acadia was walking up the stairs. I followed her behind the curtain. She went left, onto the stage, and I went right, behind where Richmond and Selene were standing. They were poised in the wings, staring at Acadia, and didn't see me. Richmond was tapping an envelope against his thigh. Selene was twisting the recently returned ring off of her finger, grimacing as if in pain.

Acadia leaned toward the microphone. "Let's begin the awards ceremony with a minute of silence for Flynn McMaster. We all know how special he was, and his life was cut tragically short."

As the attendees went quiet to honor the author, I edged farther into the wings, where it was pitch black. I moved slowly in the darkness, my arms out in front of me so I didn't bump into anything. Everything seemed to slow down as I groped forward with hesitant steps. All I could hear was my own breathing.

When Acadia began speaking again, I sensed someone moving rapidly toward me. I couldn't get out of the way fast enough, and the shove threw me onto the ground, hard.

I scrambled to crawl forward and lurched onto Candace, wrapping my arms around her legs as she passed me.

"Look out!" I yelled.

She was thrown off balance, but still managed to swing something as she fell, and Richmond, who had twisted sideways, had a look of horror on his face in response to the sight of his colleague behind him, arm upraised.

After a loud and sickening thud, he crashed to the ground.

Chapter 20

"Richie! No!" Candace screamed and dove onto her friend, putting her hands on his head to stop the blood from flowing out of the wound she'd just created. "I didn't mean to hit you!"

Selene, who had bent over to pick up the ring she'd dropped, stood upright but, catching sight of Richmond, went pale and slid to the floor.

I dialed 911 while Acadia went over to attend to Selene. People left their tables and formed a line along the stage, pointing and speculating. I spoke with the dispatcher until I felt someone remove the phone from my hand.

Lex gave me a nod and took over—bless him—while I stumbled over to the hay bales and sank down on one.

Officers burst through the back of the barn and ushered the gawking crowd out the front doors in an orderly fashion.

Candace was taken out in handcuffs. She was screeching and kicking at the officers, who stoically escorted her.

Selene was comforted and led away by Simone.

The paramedics arrived, did what they could for Richmond, and took him away to the hospital. He hadn't regained consciousness, but he was still alive.

For now.

*   *   *

Lex brought me to the Stonedale police station, a three-story rectangular building that had a pleasant facade of red brick and arched windows. I knew from previous visits to meet Lex that while the outside retained its historical charm, the inside was as modern as any university lab, with technology everywhere, from the security cameras to the computers everywhere you looked.

We passed the main counter, saying hello to Marcie, the officer who buzzed us through the locked door into a large room with desks in two neat rows and offices along both walls. I tried to get Lex to slow down and talk to me for a second, but he said we needed to hurry. We stopped in his unadorned office so that he could grab a file out of the battered black cabinet, then he led me through some hallways into a room with a rectangular pane along one side.

Candace was seated at a long table in the next room, staring directly at us. It was eerie, though I was pretty sure she couldn't see through the glass.

"That's a one-way mirror, right?"

"Yes. Keep a close eye on how she responds, physically as well as verbally."

"I can watch?"

"This time," he said. "We're not going to make a habit of it, Lila. But the chief—"

"Yes, I said so." Chief Cortez walked into the room. He was slightly taller than I was, and his dark wavy hair was shot with gray. He extended his arm and gave my hand a firm shake. Like the other officers, he was wearing a blue uniform that had a nametag below a flag pin. All of them had a badge on the other side as well, but his had an extra bar with "Police Chief" engraved in bold letters. The small paunch above his belt did nothing to lessen his authority—in fact, it gave him a certain kind of solidity. "Hello, Dr. Maclean. We meet again."

I said hello and thanked him for inviting me to consult.

"You've been most helpful," he said, giving me a wide smile. "Archer here has kept me posted. We're grateful. Now, let's get going."

The chief and I watched as Lex went into the next room. Another detective—I presumed—followed soon afterwards, carrying two cups of coffee. He offered one to Candace, who refused, then handed it to Lex.

Lex sat down across from her at the scarred wooden table. They went through her rights again to be sure she understood them, then did some paperwork and checked all the necessary information in her file to be sure it was accurate. Throughout, Candace remained calm and polite. It was a complete 180-degree turn from the agitated woman they'd dragged from the barn a little while ago. She must have realized that she was in serious trouble.

"Why don't you tell me what happened?" he began.

"When?"

"Let's start with tonight. Why did you hit Richmond?"

She flinched, as if the words were too blunt. "I didn't mean to." Tears glistened in her eyes. "I love him."

"You're in love with him?" Lex made a note.

"No. I love him. He's been a true friend."

"If he's your friend, why did you hit him with..." he flipped through some papers, "a pipe?"

"Yes, it was a pipe. It was all I could find groping around in the wings. But I wasn't trying to hit him. I was trying to hit *her*." She sat back in her chair and crossed her arms.

"Selene?" Lex asked, quietly.

"Yes," she hissed, her face contorted.

"Why?"

"Because she gets everything she wants!" Candace yelled.

"And someone had to put an end to it!"

"I hear you." Lex put both of his palms up. "Let's slow things down."

"I was aiming for her. But then Selene bent down and I hit him instead. I couldn't stop the swing. Is he okay? He's not dead, is he?" She bit her lip.

"I don't know anything yet."

She dropped her arms and leaned forward. "You should really check into Selene. She's the one who killed Flynn."

Lex froze. "Why would she kill him?"

"Because she was sleeping with him." She lifted her chin. "I found her ring in Flynn's room."

"What were you doing there?"

"Talking to him. He was in love with her."

So far, she was repeating what she'd told us at dinner. But I knew that wasn't true. I hadn't had a chance to tell Lex yet. On the way over, he'd been on the phone with the chief. When I'd tried to tell him my idea just now, he'd hurried me along.

"Just check that shovel," Candace said. "You'll find her fingerprints all over it."

Lex cut his eyes to the other detective, who took over asking questions, and left the room.

The door to our room opened.

"She brought up the shovel," he said, slapping the folder down on the table behind us. "We didn't publicize the murder weapon."

"The people on the tour saw it," I pointed out. "It could have gotten back to her a million different ways. I don't think that was much of a secret."

He thought about this.

"I bet you won't find Selene's fingerprints all over it. Candace is just trying to throw Selene under the bus. But I do have an idea about something you could ask her."

Lex paused. "Tell me."

"Here's my theory: Candace was having an affair with Flynn."

"Flynn who was having an affair with Selene?"

"Yes."

"Wait." He crossed his arms and stroked his chin as he processed the information. "You're saying that Flynn was having affairs with *both* Candace and Selene."

I nodded vigorously. "I think Ellis found out and threatened to tell her husband. She said that their families vacationed together, right? So it could follow that the husbands were close friends."

"With you so far," Lex said. "Go on."

"But *then* Candace realized that Flynn was sleeping with Selene too, when she found the engagement ring. I don't think she knew about it until this weekend. And not only did Candace realize that he was cheating on her with Selene, but that he *loved* Selene. Not her."

"Why do you think he loved Selene?"

"Because that's what Candace reported at dinner. She used *Flynn's* words to try and break up Beckett and Selene. But that wasn't all she wanted to accomplish. She'd already killed Flynn—and she wanted Selene dead too. She wanted revenge on the woman who stole her lover."

"You found all that out at dinner?"

"Never let it be said that conference banquets are boring."

"Why wouldn't she wait until later?"

"I don't know. She snapped?"

"I see. Why did *you* go backstage?"

"She had become absolutely enraged at dinner, and when I saw her following the twins, I had a feeling she was going to do something awful."

"Do you have any evidence?" Lex asked.

"I'm sure everyone at the table can back up what was said at dinner. And Selene had emailed Candace's husband Robert and told him she was cheating with Ellis. I overheard Candace reassuring him on the phone that the rumor wasn't true."

"Selene didn't know it was Flynn that Candace was involved with?" Chief Cortez asked.

"No, she thought it was Ellis. So Candace could go on loudly and truthfully proclaiming that it was false, because they said the wrong person's name."

"How did you figure this out?" Lex said, tilting his head.

"Overhearing the phone call was the last piece of the puzzle. After dinner, I was thinking over everything that had happened and it all came together in a rush...like when you're writing a literature paper."

"Um...we don't *do* that." Lex said. "Write literature papers."

"But you do gather evidence and see how it fits together."

"Yes, we do."

"It's basically the same thing."

The detective and the chief conferred with a glance. An almost imperceptible dip of the head granted Lex permission to return to the other room. It was fascinating to watch them make a decision without ever saying a word.

Lex skillfully asked more questions. At first, she denied having an affair with Flynn, but the more he stressed the logic of the connections, the less she tried to refute facts.

Finally, she looked at him wearily and said, "I've made a mess of things, haven't I?"

"Those words are haunting me," I said to Lex as he drove back to the Tattered Star Ranch. "'I've made a mess of things.' She certainly has. Two lives ended. Maybe three—have you heard anything about Richmond?"

"Right before we left, Marcie handed me a message. They're keeping him for observation overnight. They've stitched up his wound, but his skull is—miraculously—not broken. Not even cracked. Your grabbing onto Candace's legs probably saved him."

I closed my eyes and sent up thanks. "Thank goodness. Will he be okay in the long run?"

"The test results suggest he will recover quickly."

"Can he have visitors?"

"Meredith is there, but I think we should let Richmond sleep." He glanced at the dashboard. "It's almost two a.m. We'll find out more in the morning and make sure he's taken care of."

"Sounds good."

Minutes later, we parked the car in the lot and went upstairs. I collapsed on the bed in my clothes and was asleep before he turned out the light.

So much for my vision of dancing beneath the stars.

But knowing the murderer was in custody made up for it.

Chapter 21

On Sunday morning, Lex, Calista, Nate, and I shared a table in the hotel restaurant.

"The Path's End is a perfect name," I murmured. Everything seemed so peaceful now: the fountain burbling merrily in the background, the sun streaming in through the windows, my friends around the table.

"Can't believe we made it through this conference," Calista agreed.

Lex and I exchanged glances.

"I meant that we'd reached the end of the case," I clarified. "But conference works too."

She looked at me, surprised. "What happened? Who did it?"

Lex walked them through what had transpired at the police station.

Calista smiled. "Lila solves another case! That's amazing. Maybe detective work is your true calling."

"No. Lex is the authentic detective. I'm just a helper," I said, leaning against him slightly. Then I straightened up. It felt strange to snuggle with Lex in front of Nate all of a sudden.

But Nate didn't blink an eye. "You get folks to open up to you, for one thing, and you're also good at figuring out people's secrets." He waved his fork in a circle. "And we already established that you've got a gift for finding bodies."

"Don't say that, please." I shivered.

He continued undeterred. "Those are all special skills that would come in handy if you decided to take up law enforcement."

"True," Calista said. "And just think: there wouldn't be stacks of papers always waiting to be graded in police work."

"There's plenty of other paperwork." Lex lifted his mug and winked at me. "Oh, and speaking of paper, that note you pinched, with the handwriting sample? It was a match. Candace did write it. Good tip, Lila. Even though it broke every rule of evidence we have."

"You can teach me the rest. And then we could open our own agency. You up for it? Big sign that says Archer and Maclean on the door?"

"I'm up for it." He took a sip of coffee and waggled an imaginary cigar. "You've got the goods, Professor."

"That would be a great name for a television show," Calista said, sliding into dramatic voiceover mode. "Next week, on *Archer and Maclean*: the case of the cursed conference!"

"And like any good television show, there was no shortage of suspects," Nate said.

"So many scholars behaving badly," Calista agreed. "Higher than usual amount of malicious intent around here this weekend, wouldn't you say?"

We were commenting on the truth of that when I registered movement in my peripheral vision. Simone Raleigh was in the doorway of the restaurant, beckoning me over.

"Excuse me," I said.

"Where are you going?" Calista pointed to my plate. "You didn't even make a dent in your fruit and yogurt."

As I stood, I slid my eyes sideways to point toward Simone without being obvious about it.

Calista turned to look, then gave a little wave to our

colleague. So much for not being obvious. "What's going on?" she asked out of the corner of her mouth.

"No idea." I pushed my chair in and told everyone I'd be back soon.

By the time I reached the lobby, Simone was tapping her foot, but she smiled. "Lila, I owe you an apology."

I was stunned.

She clasped her hands. "What you said last night—well, it gave me pause. Maybe I haven't been fair to you. Maybe I misjudged you. Maybe I need to try harder."

I wasn't sure what all those maybes were doing in there, but I didn't want to interrupt her flow. "That's very—"

"And most of all, I need to know that I can absolutely rely on your discretion about what I told you on the terrace. I should never have carried on about private family business. And I can guarantee that the help my sister needs will be provided to her."

Ah, now I understood. She wasn't apologizing with any amount of sincerity—she hadn't actually said "I'm sorry" at all in there, I realized. She was simply trying to keep me quiet. Too little, too late.

"I understand what you're saying, Simone."

She scanned my face and recognized that no additional assurances would be forthcoming. "I appreciate that."

Selene marched across the lobby toward us. Her salmon-colored jacket was nothing like Simone's teal one—and instead of high heels, she was wearing mules.

"Hello, Lila," she said, looking down her nose at me before sweeping past with her suitcase.

She didn't even acknowledge her sister.

Who didn't acknowledge her either.

The twins appeared to be at war.

If scientists could have figured out a way to bottle the antagonism between sisters at that moment, they could have powered entire cities with it for centuries.

"Is there anything else?" I asked Simone, who was glaring after her sibling.

"No, thank you," she said tightly.

As I turned to go, I thought I saw disappointment on her face. It probably surprised me even more than it did her when I heard myself blurt out an invitation to join us.

Her face lit up. "Really?"

I nodded.

She had just bit her lip, deciding, when Beckett walked up. We exchanged greetings and he asked Simone if she could spare a few moments to chat.

She began to glow.

"Excuse me, Lila," she said to me. "Beckett and I need to speak. Rain check?"

"Rain check," I said.

Simone threaded her arm through Beckett's in a possessive manner and they strolled off together.

That whole relationship was very complicated in theory, I knew, but it didn't look so complicated right now.

As I crossed the lobby on my way back to the restaurant, someone tapped me on the shoulder. I turned to find Sunny at my elbow, bouncing on her heels. She had a big bow on the back of her head like an oversized doll and was once again dressed in yellow to match her name, as she'd explained was her habit to the tour group during some point on our ill-fated march through the property.

"This is for you," she said, thrusting a wad of cloth toward me. "Courtesy of Tattered Star Ranch Tours."

I accepted the lump of white fabric. "What is it?"

She giggled and covered her mouth, removing her fingers long enough to squeak, "Read it!"

I shook it out and held up a t-shirt that said *I Got Freezer*

Burn at the Ranch.

Although Sunny was still consumed by mirth, she managed to unpeel her fingers from her heavily frosted lips. "Don't you *adore* it?"

"Um—thank you."

"These shirts were my idea." She informed me that anyone who got locked in the freezer received one of these and that they were highly prized, even considered collector's items by movie fans. "They trade them online. In forums and such."

"But if the t-shirts are collector's items, doesn't that encourage people to lock themselves in the freezer on purpose?" I wondered aloud.

She stopped bouncing and drew her over-plucked eyebrows together. "I never thought about that before." After a moment, she brightened and shooed the issue away with both hands. "That's a problem for another day. Enjoy your shirt and come visit us again soon." I took that as my cue to leave, thanked her again, and returned to my friends.

At the table, I shoved the shirt into my bag—no need to relive the whole freezer ordeal right now. Especially since Candace had confessed to that too. The way she'd described it to Lex, she had been racing through the woods after "taking care of Flynn"—her euphemism—when she saw me at the edge of the freezer through the open slaughterhouse door. She'd hoped that veering a few steps off the path to administer a swift shove would be enough to lock me inside where no one would find me, thereby putting an end to what she called my "incessant questioning."

Whatever.

I had just taken a bite of yogurt when Meredith approached us, out of breath. "Sorry, I had to run over because I didn't know if you were done eating. And I definitely didn't want to miss you."

I made sure everyone had been introduced, invited her to join us, and asked about Richmond.

"He's doing well—thank you for asking. We're going to stay in Colorado for a while before we fly back so that he can rest, but he's not feeling up to having visitors, I'm afraid."

"We understand. Please give him our best. And if you're interested in getting together next week, we'll be here. We'd love to take you out for dinner or something."

"I'll tell him. In fact, I come on his behalf."

She put her glasses on top of her head and rooted around in her shoulder bag, then handed me a tan manila envelope. "Please open it."

I slid my thumb along the flap and pulled out a sheet of paper with a border of gold. I skimmed the words, and as I realized what I was reading, I put my hand over my mouth and raised my head, locking eyes with Meredith.

"What?" Lex looked back and forth between us.

"This says—no! Is it true, Meredith?"

She nodded, smiling.

"This says I won the New Voices Prize!"

"Congratulations," Lex said, clapping so loudly that the diners at nearby tables peered at us curiously.

"But I thought Richmond wanted to give it to the Raleighs."

"He did at first," Meredith said, "but that was outrageous and he knew it. Both Candace and I thought you had the best proposal, and once we presented our arguments to him, he agreed."

Calista grabbed my hands. "I *knew* you would win."

"I didn't know!" I gasped. "I never even imagined it."

"So proud of you, cousin."

"It had to be unanimous," Meredith informed us. "Not an easy feat."

"Thank you. Please thank the press too. I'm so grateful."

Lex smiled. "You won fair and square, Professor."

I just sat there, clutching the certificate.

"Well, show it to me already." He stretched his hand across the table, reviewed it, and gave me a wink. "Well done."

He passed it to Nate, who congratulated me and handed it to my cousin.

"I'm so glad you're happy, Lila." Meredith said. "Sorry you didn't get to cross the stage and have it announced in front of everyone. In all the madness last night, nothing was given out. All the winners in the various categories are being notified by email. Not quite the same thing."

"I don't care about that. This is a genuine thrill."

"If Lila won, why was Selene onstage last night?" Calista asked Meredith.

My editor smiled. "Oh, Selene wasn't up there as a winner. She was going to thank everyone for looking for her ring before Richmond took over the microphone." Something flickered across Meredith's face, causing her pleasant expression to fade. Her sense of unease reached me before her words did. "But Lila, could we please talk somewhere privately?"

This wasn't going to be good.

"I trust everyone here," I said, gesturing around the table. "You can speak freely."

"I'm sorry to have to tell you this. Especially right now. But while you are indeed the winner of the award, we're not going to publish your book after all."

Calista gasped.

Meredith looked stricken. "Oh, that came out wrong. Let me try again. It's not just your book. We're not going to be publishing *anyone's* books. The press is closing."

"Oh no. Why?" I struggled to catch my breath as the implications crowded in. Goodbye, book. Which meant goodbye, tenure. Which meant I'd need to find a new job. Which meant

I'd need to move somewhere else. Which meant I'd be leaving everyone I loved here. I pushed that anxiety spiral away from me with a concerted effort and tried to concentrate on her words.

"The university, frankly, is horrified by the negative publicity that has been generated by the conference, from which we were meant to come home victorious, having launched the new critical guide series and new award to national applause. Instead, we lost Ellis and Flynn, Richmond is hurt, Candace is going to be locked up, and let's not forget Flynn's keynote speech discrediting the series, which went viral. They're not saying it outright—we were given a byzantine tale about sudden but necessary redistribution of funding, but long story short: it's over."

I was spinning. From the highest peak to the lowest point in the valley in seconds flat.

"I'm very sorry," I managed to say.

"No. Lila, I am. And I'm horrified to have to deliver this news, especially this late in the process. But I hope you know that your work is extremely good. You'll be able to find a new home for it, I'm sure."

"You will," said Nate firmly.

"No question." Calista added.

Lex nodded in agreement.

"I genuinely wish you the best." Meredith apologized again. "Forgive me?"

"Of course. Nothing to forgive."

"These things happen, though I'm heartbroken that it's happening to you. Keep in touch, okay?" She gave me an awkward hug and walked away.

The thought of having to find another publisher hit me hard, and my eyes welled up. I wiped a tear away quickly, but the woman passing me with her tray saw it anyway.

"Are you all right, my dear?" Bibi Callahan set the tray on the table next to me and bent down to peer into my face.

"I'm fine," I said. "Thank you."

"Well, clearly you are *not* fine," she said. "Does this have something to do with the way you dove onto that wild woman last night and prevented a catastrophe?"

I laughed. "Not really, but thank you for that description."

"I mean it. You're my hero."

I waved at an empty chair. "Would you like to join us?"

"I would, but just briefly. I need to get going soon. My friend Pat's driving, and she's a stickler for being on time."

"Now," she said, once she was settled and I'd made introductions again. "What's all this about?"

"I found out that my publisher is closing."

"Oh, you can't publish your book with them? I was so looking forward to reading it. That's too bad, dear." Her green eyes shone with sympathy. As a retired professor, the meaning of the situation was not lost on her. "Have you sent it out to other publishers?"

"I have. Since Isabella only wrote three novels and they were in limited distribution, they haven't heard about her enough to know how fantastic she is. Which is ironic, because once people know about her, they'll love her." I began musing aloud—I couldn't seem to stop myself. "Maybe I need to find a way to offer them more, see if I can find some letters she wrote or something. I have a sabbatical coming up next fall. I'll just have to look harder." I stopped. The whole idea made me dizzy.

"Your school offers a sabbatical *before* you apply for tenure?"

"Just one semester. They want us to have time to research."

"What a lovely idea. Many don't, until afterwards."

"We feel very fortunate."

"I should expect so. Are you going somewhere?"

"I was going to stay with my mother in New York, but…"

She nodded. "Your mother?"

"Yes, she's an artist. Violet O."

Her eyes widened. "Why, I adore her work. She's your mother? What a small world. We're friends. Well, not exactly friends. Friendly, perhaps."

That didn't surprise me. My mother knew everyone. "You are? Where did you meet?"

"I compared her work to that of several postmodern poets in a paper at a conference back east. She was attending the conference, happened to hear about it from members of the audience, and invited me for a drink. We had a terrific talk and have kept in touch on social media since then."

"I love that. Anyway, she's hosting an art-in, so there's no place for me."

"An art-in?"

"Where she and a small group of her friends lock themselves away from the world for several months and create art and hold workshops and have power circles and all sorts of re-energizing things. They rotate locations every couple of years, and it's her turn to host. They'd made the plans long before I knew I'd be taking a sabbatical."

"I see. That sounds marvelous, to be honest. I do miss the east coast. But I have a different idea. Use my guest cottage. You're welcome to it any time you like. It's very quiet. Superb for reading and writing."

I stared at her.

"Obviously, you could come and go as you please. It's not too far from Stonedale, but it would allow you real space to focus on your work. Believe me, I've learned from experience that if you're on sabbatical but hover near campus, people have a way of finding you. That will interrupt your concentration and impede your progress."

"What a nice offer! But I couldn't afford to—"

She laughed softly at that. "You wouldn't have to pay me anything at all. I'd be glad for the company. Though I wouldn't be pestering you all day, promise. I'm working on my own book." She cocked her head slightly. "If you needed a break, however, perhaps you could help me go through some files, if you have a mind to do so. My study is a mess, and I've been meaning to organize it for years."

I hesitated. Was I really thinking about entering an arrangement with a professor I'd met for two seconds at a conference? Still, there was something honest and forthright about her. I was drawn to her kindness. And I could always check in with my mother beforehand, who apparently knew her.

"I'd be happy to help you organize your study," I said.

"You might find something useful in my papers. I taught American Literature too. And I have an extensive library of mysteries. That's an affinity I believe we both share, judging from your presentation." Her eyes twinkled.

"How exciting! Thank you for your generosity."

"It's settled, then." She clapped her hands. "We'll have a wonderful time."

I smiled at her. "Looking forward to it."

She paused. "Having attended your panel, I suppose I should clarify one thing, so that we have no secrets between us." Bibi leaned forward. "My married name is Bibi Callahan, but my maiden name is Isabella Dare."

Photo by Angela Kleinsasser

Cynthia Kuhn

Cynthia Kuhn is an English professor and author of the Lila Maclean Academic Mysteries: *The Semester of Our Discontent, The Art of Vanishing, The Spirit in Question,* and *The Subject of Malice.* Her work has also appeared in *McSweeney's Quarterly Concern, Literary Mama, Copper Nickel, Prick of the Spindle, Mama PhD,* and other publications. Honors include an Agatha Award (Best First Novel), William F. Deeck-Malice Domestic Grant, and Lefty Award nominations (Best Humorous Mystery). Originally from upstate New York, she lives in Colorado with her family. For more information, please visit cynthiakuhn.net.

**The Lila Maclean Academic Mystery Series
by Cynthia Kuhn**

Henery Press Mystery Books

And finally, before you go...
Here are a few other mysteries
you might enjoy:

THE HOUSE ON HALLOWED GROUND

Nancy Cole Silverman

A Misty Dawn Mystery (#1)

When Misty Dawn, a former Hollywood Psychic to the Stars, moves into an old craftsman house, she encounters the former owner, the recently deceased Hollywood set designer, Wilson Thorne. Wilson is unaware of his circumstances, and when Misty explains the particulars of his limbo state, and how he might help himself if he helps her, he's not at all happy. That is until young actress Zoey Chamberlain comes to Misty's door for help.

Zoey has recently purchased The Pink Mansion and thinks it's haunted. But when Misty searches the house, it's not a ghost she finds, but a dead body. The police suspect Zoey, but Zoey fears the death may have been a result of the ghost...and a family curse. Together Misty and Wilson must untangle the secrets of The Pink Mansion or submit to the powers of the family curse.

Available at booksellers nationwide and online

Visit www.henerypress.com for details

MURDER ON A SILVER PLATTER

Shawn Reilly Simmons

A Red Carpet Catering Mystery (#1)

Penelope Sutherland and her Red Carpet Catering company just got their big break as the on-set caterer for an upcoming blockbuster. But when she discovers a dead body outside her house, Penelope finds herself in hot water. Things start to boil over when serious accidents threaten the lives of the cast and crew. And when the film's star, who happens to be Penelope's best friend, is poisoned, the entire production is nearly shut down.

Threats and accusations send Penelope out of the frying pan and into the fire as she struggles to keep her company afloat. Before Penelope can dish up dessert, she must find the killer or she'll be the one served up on a silver platter.

Available at booksellers nationwide and online

Visit www.henerypress.com for details

NOT A CREATURE WAS STIRRING

Christina Freeburn

A Merry & Bright Handcrafted Mystery (#1)

Empty nester Merry Winters loves three things: Christmas, crafting and her family. To regain purpose and joy, Merry hits the road to a Christmas vendor event with her furry sidekick Ebenezer in her new mobile crafting sleigh, aka an RV.

But it soon turns into the nightmare before Christmas when Merry unwraps her Scrooge of an ex-husband's body in one of the RV's compartments. Add to that his missing winning lottery ticket believed to be stashed somewhere in the RV, leading the homicide detective and Merry's stepdaughter to believe Merry is the one whodunit.

With visions of prison dancing in her head, will Merry be able to solve this Christmas calamity before she's locked away?

Available at booksellers nationwide and online

Visit www.henerypress.com for details

STAGING IS MURDER

Grace Topping

A Laura Bishop Mystery (#1)

Laura Bishop just nabbed her first decorating commission—staging a 19th-century mansion that hasn't been updated for decades. But when a body falls from a laundry chute and lands at Laura's feet, replacing flowered wallpaper becomes the least of her duties.

To clear her assistant of the murder and save her fledgling business, Laura's determined to find the killer. Turns out it's not as easy as renovating a manor home, especially with two handsome men complicating her mission: the police detective on the case and the real estate agent trying to save the manse from foreclosure.

Worse still, the meddling of a horoscope-guided friend, a determined grandmother, and the local funeral director could get them all killed before Laura props the first pillow.

Available at booksellers nationwide and online

Visit www.henerypress.com for details

CPSIA information can be obtained
at www.ICGtesting.com
Printed in the USA
LVHW051343220422
716950LV00023B/1526